THE TEENAGE WORRIER'S Guide to

LIFE

Ros Asquith

as Letty Chubb

THE TEENAGE WORRIER'S GUIDE TO LIFE
A CORGI BOOK : 0 552 14534 3

First publication in Great Britain

PRINTING HISTORY
Corgi edition published 1997

5 7 9 10 8 6

Copyright © 1997 by Ros Asquith

The right of Ros Asquith to be identified as the author of this work has
been asserted in accordance with the Copyright Designs and Patents Act
1988

Set in 11½pt Linotype Garamond by Phoenix Typesetting, Ilkley,
West Yorkshire

Corgi Books are published by Transworld Publishers Ltd,
61–63 Uxbridge Road, London W5 5SA,
in Australia by Transworld Publishers,
c/o Random House Australia Pty Ltd,
20 Alfred Street, Milsons Point, NSW 2061,
in New Zealand by Transworld Publishers,
c/o Random House New Zealand,
18 Poland Road, Glenfield, Auckland,
and in South Africa by Transworld Publishers,
c/o Random House (Pty) Ltd,
Endulini, 5a Jubilee Road, Parktown 2193.

Printed and bound in Great Britain by
Cox & Wyman Ltd, Reading, Berkshire.

Tear-stained pillow
Unmade bed
Cranny of cheerless roomlet
Apology-for-a-dwelling
Trivial town
Minuscule nation
Tragic Werld
Lilliputian speck in Solar System
Paltry dot in Yuniverse
Cosmos
The Great Be Ond

Dear Teenage Worrier(s),

This volume, the — er — biggest and best El Chubb extravaganza to date (chance-would-be-a-fine-thing-I-should-be-so-lucky-and-other-assorted-clichés) will encompass the Meaning of LIFE, the True Nachur of Existence, the opposite of Banana, Being and Nothingness Etck in all its myriad diversity. As you may have noticed from my address, above, I have not yet banished all traces of Fear, Worry, Glume and Dume from my psyche. I am certain, however, that, by sharing with you (dear caring Reader) my innermost forebodings and translating them into a rich and meaningful tapestry, together we can conquer the werld and make loads of dosh (I mean, improve the environment for future generations so that yumanity can co-habit peacefully in this Earthly Paradise, Etck).

Teenage Worriers looking for information on how to embezzle, bonk and get free drugs would be better off dipping into MPs' memoirs or hanging around the House of Common behaviour. Similarly, fresh-faced Teenage Worriers hoping for a buke about gung-ho items like Gurl Guides or abseiling will feel only a brief frisson of disappointment at the brevity of the entries on these subjects — as they will instead be plunged into a Voyage of the Soul (ahem) that will make the Celestine Prophecy seem like Little Noddy.

Er, at least, that's my humble plan . . .

I have chosen as my, um, theme, more or less everything. We Teenage Worriers spend roughly 8 hours of each 24 in bed (OK, let's admit 14 hours for depressives, 3 hours for ravers), 7 hours at skule (we assume), leaving 9 hours in which to file nails, nail files, pick noses, yawn, dream how to make the 14 hours spent in bed — complete with snoring siblings, raging elders, putrefying socks — more exciting (I mean useful). Etck.

First, may I humbly thank you for the mountain of Lurve-mail in response to my previous humble tomes. These heartfelt missives, added to the skyscrapers of old newspapers, DIY volumes and remnants of unfinished novel belonging to my Adored Father, have caused my Only Mother to consider moving out before she is engulfed by what was once, as she so reprovingly admonishes, a rainforest.

All of which has led me to scribble this on the backs of envelopes, junk mail, red telephone bills Etck in order to avoid More Guilt and, dare I say it? WORRY. For if writing my insignificant contributions to the mental health of the generation that will one day be ruling this Noble

*Planet is causing an eco-disaster, then should I be allowed
even to disturb the ether?*

*Sometimes I think that instead of being a nun I should
become a Jayne. These are V. Religious Indian folk who
wear masks so that they don't breathe in minute insects,
and sweep the floor in front of them wherever they go so
they do not tread on same. This also leads them to respect
the lives of rats Etck who spread rather a lot of diseases
and therefore help to kill rather a lot of Jaynes. Life is a
hall of mirrors, they say, and it's all a question of balance.*

*What differentiates TEENAGE WORRIERS from
other yuman inhabitants of Planet Earth (and places us in
much the same camp as household pets, and with similarly
varying degrees of charm and temper, is our lack of*

a) Autonomy and
b) Finance.

*For these we remain sullenly dependent on our parents
(social workers, uncaring Irresponsible Adults, Etck),
artificially tied to the bosom of the family (if we are lucky
enough to have a family, lash, guilt, always someone worse
off than you Etck) while our hormones are moaning 'Freeee
me! Freeee me! Let me roam freeeee!' and the Child
Within weeps 'Want a hot choccy!' Viz: Cause of most of
conflict in home and much of conflict in World-at-Large
(NB Odd phrase that makes the planet sound like a
criminal).*

*I V. Much hope the guide to LIFE will enable the
average Teenage Worrier to find ways of making the 9*

'Leisure' hours (plus weekends, holidays and the yawning abyss of the post-skule future) a profound and meaningful experience.

And now, forward to pastures new (ish)! Turn yourself from a dume-laden glume-maiden into a frolicsome filly flicking your fetlocks at the Yuniverse! (NB Boyz turn into proud colts flaring nostrils and arching noble forelocks Etck). LIFE would be much easier, I often ponder, if whole Yuman Race was transformed into horses. That Jonathan Swift had the right idea when he wrote Gulliver's Travels and made the horses V. Noble and the people crazed ravening beasts intent only on guzzling, biffing and bonking. How I long for a more Spiritooal existence (ahem).

Lurve,

Letty Chubb

N.B. There are some helpline numbers at the v. back of this buke.

(x x)

HERE IS A BRIEF UPDATE ON MY LIFE . . .

UPDATE . . . MOI.

SCARELET (interesting Freudian slip, must explore festering soul to uncover Hidden Agenda) – I mean, of course, SCARLETT JANE CHUBB or LETTY (it is NO fun being called Scarlett unless you look like flame-haired temptress crossed with vixen-from-hell).

I thought gurlz were supposed to stop growing at 15 or so, but it seems I am becoming more of a leaning tower of Pisa by the minute (whereas my little brother remains a bouncing sphere of Pizza). Those of you who are vertically challenged, however, should not feel envy, as I do not have the willowy grace of supermodel but more the aspect of a street lamp struck by a heavy goods vehicle from which citizens flee in terror of imminent collapse.

Hair still the colour of that bread that well-meaning middle-class mothers try to force down their infants when all the babas want is nice, pale, bouncy, ready-sliced foam. If my hair were only like rats' tails I wouldn't mind, but it is more like a Gorgon's wig with the texture of brambles. (Not that appearances are important to *moi*, merely vital.)

Good news : I think my nose has stopped growing. I haven't measured it for two days now but I *sense* a new stability . . . maybe I won't have to hire myself out as the Yuman Vacuum Cleaner after all.

Craters, spots and cold sores still chase each other like storm clouds over my mug, each battling for ascendancy according to ye passing seasons. The plukes are no respecters of the time of year, however, popping out and waving waxy tendrils whenever they spot a cleft-chinned wunderbabe approaching. Since the CCW is never looking at *moi* anyway, but always at my mate Hazel, this makes little difference to the well of loneliness I inhabit. (Cue banshees, violins.)

I am still planning to be a film director (having postponed my Spiritooal Desire to be a Nun and give up Sins of Flesh – not that I have, yet, tragickly had opportunity to experience said Sins) and have enrolled on a film course one evening a week, starting tomorrow. Who knows what great opportunities to meet V. Handsome – I mean V. Interllekshual – boyz, lie ahead!

I have completely relinquished my passion for Daniel Hope.

No.

I must be honest with you.

If I cannot be honest with you, then what hope is there for newshounds, teachers, lawyers, Werld Leaders to be honest? What hope for Werld Peace? Ecological Sanity? Future of our generation Etckh? Zzzzzzzzzzzzzzzzzzzzz . . .

Sorry, dropped off to sleep for a minute. What I mean to say is, I do still carry a torch for D. Hope. I know I shouldn't. I know he's a rat who has abandoned me for two of my BEST FRENDZ. But that's how it is. Luckily, the torch is burning V. Low, sputtering, and could be snuffed out V. Kwick if someone tall, dark and handsome enough (I mean caring, sharing, and kind enough) came along to win my heart. Readers, if you have a spare brother out there, post him to me special delivery.

All right, I'll admit it. There is Someone Else in my life.

Or at least, in my Imagination.

And it just so happens that he is enrolled in the film course too. That is NOT the reason I enrolled. As you know, I have always had ambitions to be a film director. But, well, it isn't entirely a coincidence. In fact my frend Aggy pointed him out to me. He has just moved into the neighbourhood. One of her zillions of brothers told Aggy he was going on the course. Ahem. The Cat is now out of the Bag. I would have enrolled anyway. Honest.

More about **Adam Stone** (swoooooooooon, hope his heart isn't like his surname Etck) later . . .

UPDATE . . . MOTHER
Alice Constance Gosling

My Mother is V. V. Anxious to give up her job at the kiddies' library. She complains of Falling Standards, is fed up that all the boyz want to do is take out Batman comcs, football annuals Etck and that all the gurlz want is V. Soppy romances about poor heroines called Sarah who get off with cleft-chinned hunks with polo-sticks, country houses, minions Etck. I say, in what way does that differ from an adults' library? Anyway, I saw her hiding a copy of *Passion among the Peonies* under her pillow only last week, so I reckon she is V. Two faced and snobby about this, though you would think a well-bred girl like her wld at least choose an author who could spell ponies right.

The lengths I have to go to to get attention
from my Only Mother...

She is, as ever, distraught about our Edukashun,
believing (possibly rightly) that I have no chance of
any of the magic A–C grades at Sluggs
Comprehensive with its 'lively mix' of 85% free
school dinners. Since Aggy is one of that 85% and
also the cleverest Teenager in the Yuniverse, I feel
somewhat ratty about these statistics and believe
that they do not give a true and accurate version
Etck of Real Werld. But Sluggs is desperately trying
to beat league tables by expelling everyone in sight,
cramming borderline pupils to get 'C' grades and
abandoning all below.

Since I sadly cling to flimsy life-raft of middle-
class values, held afloat by pushy parents Etck I'll
probably scrape through, waving to less fortunate
classmates drowning in rocky seas of discrimination,
hurtling over cliffs of unemployment Etck just
because they didn't get help with course work or
live in nice areas with lawns and roses round door
Etck. Mind you, I wish I did.

Meanwhile my Only Mother weeps over Lost
Opportunities like the poor student she forsook for
the promising, young, angry, Romantick, Working
Class Novelist who became my Father. The poor
student, Neville, founded a komputer empire and
now jets between his 6 houses, spending most of his
time on a remote Caribbean Isle . . .

Another Deep Regret is that she abandoned her
Art to raise her family. While I proudly support
feminist values Etck I cannot help thinking my

Only Mother might have been happier if she could have put just a teensy bit of her Artistick Temperament into ye simple values of Home-making. Like occasionally cooking something edible. Or ironing her children's T-shirts (just now and then is all I ask). Or redecorating a room instead of squandering her wages on oil paint. I am V. fed up with the nursery rhyme freeze in my room now.

My Mother's latest Wild Ruse to get hold of some dosh is to spend what little she has on a komputer graphics course. She says this will enable her to get jobz on Posh Magz. I don't like to tell her that the staff of those magz are all about 12. I am a bit Worried she may have an Ulterior Motive for her course (like I do about mine, ahem) and am keeping a Beady Eye on the Adult Edukashun Institute just In Case . . .

UPDATE . . . FATHER
Leonard Anthony Chubb

My Adored Father still writes Do-It-Yourself articles (based on his own tragick experiments in Home Improvement), plays komputer games (invented by Neville, the poor student my mother spurned, and thus rubbing salt in Only Mother's wounds), and writes about one page of his new novel a year . . .

His first (and only) novel, *Moving On*, which made him Toast of London 22 years ago, has just been

In .Ye Chubb home.

re-issued to a wild chorus of indifference. We had champagne Etck on day of publication and waited eagerly for cheques to pour through door. But sadly not a single newspaper has reviewed it yet and my Father has spent the last week storming round bukeshops and demanding to know why they aren't stocking his Great Work. Still, it's only 6 days since the first copies came through so there is still HOPE.

Meanwhile, he languishes playing *CITYSCAPE*, in which you have to build a city in space to house yumanity after destruction of Planet Earth. New City must have abundant ozone layer, acres of parks, zero pollution Etck Etck. It is V. difficult, after you have got all the eco-factors right, to house more than about 200 people, so it is V. Elitist. But my Father is always in V. Good mood if he gets to level 2, because the komputer emits a cheering sound accompanied by a host of little green figures with pink hair who crowd on screen to award him with an encouraging message re his virtues as a Saviour. The game has 48 levels, so he has long way to go. It will have to do until he wins Booker Prize, gets a job Etck.

UPDATE . . . BROTHER 1
Ashley (18)

Interesting developments re Ashley for all those of you who have written in begging to meet this wise, witty, noble, handsome brother of mine. His posh fiancée, Caroline, has asked for a 'cooling off' period of 3 months to see if she really cares, they are too young to tie knot blah blah. Ashley is upset but, being perfect, is at Oxford knuckling down to his degree so that he can become world famous brain surgeon to the Poor-and-Needy, though maybe by the time he qualifies he'll be required to lobotomize said Poor-and-Needy to prevent Revolution Etck.

My Adored Only Parents are more distraught because although Ashley V. Young to marry, fiancée's folks are loaded, so they were hoping for weekends away on yachts. And they complain about *our* generation being materialistic, Thatcher's children Etck!

UPDATE . . . BROTHER 2
Benjy (5)

Benjy will be 6 soon, still has golden curls, eyes like forget-me-nots, cherubic mug, teeth like a piranha and a kick like a mule. He is still anguished about the floors. His latest obsession is that the mild pink bath mat is a disguised Martian that will abduct him if he is left alone in the loo.

I blame all these 'bukes that will feed his imagination' that my Mother keeps bringing back from the library. She then never has time to read them to him and he, being able only to decipher a handful of words, finds his imagination somewhat overfed. Kindly Big Sister then reads him the real story which is, I admit, usually more frightening than anything even he could dream up. He then goes to bed in tears, only to wake and plague sister with his company through rest of long night. How will I get my GCSEs under this kind of pressure? It is harrowing domestic circumstances like these that examiners never take into account . . .

If I use the ravishing purple dye I bought to jazz up my old T-shirt (having succumbed to an article in *Smirk* saying purple was the Big New Colour) to dye the bath mat, will it placate Benjy? Or will it further convince him of the alien's chameleon powers? It is such humble Worries that I hope to address as I tread the weary pages of this work . . .

UPDATE . . . PETS
Rover, Horace and Kitty

Ah. **Rover**. My Solace among the woes of this Weary World. My frend in need. Cat among Cats.

Kitty: appearance of seraph, temper of barracuda

Rover has recently perfected her art of opening fridge to the point where we now have to barricade it all times. My Father says it saves money, as no-one else uses it much any more. My cat allergy is a trifle worse, but Lurve conquers all and most of my spare money goes on flea potions for Rover rather than allergy potions for *moi*.

Benjy ditto for Kitty, above

Horace the gerbil is still revolting – I mean revolving – on wheel for eternity (I confess I am uncertain whether gerbils have souls), though Horace is not as bad as **Kitty**, my *bête noire* – or should I say *bête blanche*? Everybody (except *moi*) adores her, finding her playful kittenish ways (like when she pees in my bed, or scratches my poster of Brad Pittbull) utterly charming. As a result, Rover is losing out on Lurve from the rest of the family, being old and on scrap heap of their fleeting loyalties. I have to make up for this, but it is no hardship. True Lurve always finds a way . . .

UPDATE . . . GRANDMOTHERS

Granny Chubb still shines like a beacon as the other great Lurve of my life. Also shines glasses, windows, as despite failing sight and arthritic joints cannot give up lifelong vocation as cleaner.

I visit her postage stamp of a council flat as often as poss and get all the Lurve, comfort, biscuits, hot choccy Etck that the rest of LIFE does not proffer. It is worth donning the tangerine and lilac bolero she knitted last month to do so. It is worth listening to stories of ye World War, Grandpa Chubb, how they lived for two weeks on half a biscuit and a slice of spam because she gave all the rations to my infant Father. In fact, it is V. Interesting and I mean to use G. Chubb as subject for my heart-warming-yet-cutting-edge film about how this once Grate Nation has spurned its old folk in pursuit of ye hollow grail of profit.

My GCSE (Granny Chubb's Specs Endeavour) fund is running rather low as result of my selfish escapades and I blush to think how my LIFE savings could have bought her a decent pair of spectacles. I fear she cannot decipher the sell-by date on the tinned cat food she so eagerly consumes and will succumb to food poisoning before I have saved enough. CAMPAIGN for Free specs, eye tests Etck for pensioners!!

Grandma Gosling, my mother's mother, is still what used to be called 'a lady' in that she treats a duke and a dustman just the same, ie: abusing both in a voice like a megaphone. She has never recovered from her belief that her Adored Daughter married (huh!) beneath her (a view sadly shared, I am beginning to believe, by my disloyal Mother) and that therefore her grandchildren are little better than oiks.

UPDATE . . . FRENDZ

Aggy is still my closest frend at skule. I have completely recovered from her brief sojourn with Daniel Hope. She was, as I expected, much too brainy for him . . . though it will be V. Interesting to see who conquers werld in later life: Blond, thin, handsome, articulate, well-connected, privately educated, but – if I'm honest – only moderately

Beautiful Hazel and Brainy Aggy are still
my FAVOURITE FRENDZ

clever Daniel? or Brilliant, shy, awkward, plump,
black, poor Aggy from Sluggs Comprehensive? Send
your predictions to L. Chubb and see if we can prove
my Father is wrong to say nothing has improved
since he was a lad (violins, moan, sneaking suspicion
he may be right . . .).

I am still V. Good frendz with **Hazel**, most-
glamorous-Teenager-in-Britain. As far as I know, I
am her only confidante – as she finds the gurlz at
the posh academy she now goes to V. snooty. Also, if
any of them knew she was going out with a gurl, she
is sure they wld burn her at stake, put slugs in her
tennis shoes Etck.

But my frendship with **Sarah Spiggott (Spiggy)**
is on rocks since she sped off with Daniel Hope in
her clutches. Yes, Reader, their Lurve still blossoms
(puke) and for some reason I no longer seem able to
consider Spiggy's groovy, loose-limbed Ozzie flair as
quite suiting my tastes . . .

UPDATE . . . BOYFRENDZ

Brian Bolt

Those of you who have read too many romances
about how the loyal quiet admirer finally wins the
heroine's affections when her eyes have been opened
to his charms by the feckless behaviour of the cleft-
chinned wunderbabe she has hitherto fancied, may
have been hoping that I started to return BB's
affections. But, although his complexion has
improved and he is V. Interested in Art, I wish he
Lurved Aggy, rather than *moi*. Also, there was a
further incident, whose constituents included
custard and a pair of frogman's flippers, that I am
too embarrassed to recount.

Daniel Hope

I can't wait for Spiggy (my one-time frend) to dump
him for a surfer. When the salt tears flow from
Daniel's sapphire eyes, causing his golden hair to
curl in soft damp tendrils around his Noble Brow
(phew, pant), I shall be the first to run to comfort
him – I mean laugh scornfully, toss my proud mane
and canter off into the arms of . . .

Adam Stone

The new object of my affections has shoulders a
little too broad for perfection and hips just a mite
narrow. His legs are longer than might perfectly suit
you vertically challenged types. His eyes the colour

of midnight skies . . . his hair a dark bunch of
grapes . . . It is V. Diff for me to know what to wear
on the first evening of my film course. Must look
casual yet studious, bubbly yet sensitive. Above all,
creative. Will he notice *moi*? Sadly, Benjy overheard
me mulling this over with Aggy and suggested I go
dressed as Batman . . .

UPDATES . . . ECCENTRICITIES ETCK

I wish I could say I have managed to write the werd
that is about dying and rhymes with 'breath', but,
despite following my own excellent advice about

Trying Not to Worry, this continues to plague me. I still say 'banana' instead. I wonder if I used a different word, I might conquer this habit. Perhaps 'raincoat' would do it? Viz: 'The tragic news of her beloved's raincoat precipitated a storm of grief' or, 'Once he learned of his impending raincoat, all his hopes for the future were for ever dampened.'

No, I'll stick to banana for now, or else we'll all get confused. I still have a thing about even numbers, have to touch the floor twice if I drop something and am apt to pray loudly in stressful circumstances (I usually come to my senses if anyone appears and pretend I am rehearsing a religious play).

My fringe has grown and helps to disguise my nervous tic. I have managed to go out twice without my lucky rabbit's foot, although I admit I only got a few paces the road on each occasion before retrieving it. Still, a small step for personkind . . .

And now, on with the buke ⟶

CHAPTER ONE
AAAAAAAze

Tension is mounting re my first class on the film course. I got V. Big Buke out of library which turned out to be published before WW2 and showed ancient cameras with spools the size of tractor wheels and V. intricate sprockets, flanges, twinges, widgets, spridgets Etck. Not surprising they started off making silent movies or soundtrack would have been full of sounds of cursing, heaving, springs breaking, ligaments twanging, actors shouting to make themselves heard above din Etck.

500 pages on the development of 'talkies' and the future of colour film, though doubtless fascinating in their way, induced alternating panic attacks and prolonged bouts of snoozing. Where was the key that would unlock the door to the glamorous werld of Hollywood . . . ahem, I mean the serious, artistic, heartfelt side, of course?

Wondered briefly if I might make a splash by reinventing wheel and making V. Grainy black-and-white silent movie with lots of stills for cheapness – I mean atmosphere. Cld make powerful impression on Adam Stone, sorry, tutors, for street cred, commitment, the simple dramatic image that Says All.

Carted vast tome back to library and asked if they had biog of Tarantino, but was taken to sports section by helpful but aged librarian, clearly under impression

24

Quentin was a striker for Inter Milan and delighted by joys of Gurlz entering realms of Boyz Etck. Confusion sorted just in time to find V. Sultry Gurl with exposed navel in front of moi *taking out entire library's contemporary film section (three bukes). Begged her to let me have just one.*

'But I need it for my course,' she murmured in husky Californian tones. (I mean by this not that she is a Californian husky, but that . . . well, you know . . .) Gaaaad!

'Er, would that be the, um, New Directions course, starting Thursday week?' squeaked moi, *still hypnotized by navel, which appeared to be winking dismissively at Yrs Truely Pathetick. She undulated her neck in a manner that made her head approach the affirmative and glided out, the vast bukes seemingly weightless in her slender yet forceful grip.*

Arg! Competition so early in the game!

Raked rest of library and found Adventures of the Silver Screen *(pub. 1956),* How a Film is Made *(pub. 1954) and* Let's go to the Cinema *– all in the kiddies' section. V. Glad it wasn't my Mother's day at work in the library. Pretended to the librarian they were for small sibling. Got rather involved in* Let's Go to the Cinema, *in which a V. shy 10-year-old gurl, who lives on a V. remote Highland Island and has never seen a film, swims treacherous loch in midwinter, seething with murderous undercurrents, German submarines, flocks of Nessies, tidal waves of yuman waste Etck (I hv made up some of these bits to heighten drama) to fetch doctor for sick aunt.*

Her prize is a visit to the cinema, her first taste of the Silver Screen (popcorn also), her first vision of a world beyond her island home, blah blah. This seemed a pretty stinky sort of prize for such acts of selfless heroineism, but just the same was wiping tears from nose when realized I was hurtling through unknown territory having got on wrong bus.

Had to get two buses home. Arrived to find supper burnt to crisp in oven. Berated Only Mother who announced she was not a slave, why didn't I make supper for her now and then Etck. Why do Adults always start discussion on Meaning of Life when you want something simple like a fish finger that doesn't look like an old firework?

Cried self to sleep over Highland gurl. Woken by Benjy in throes of nightmare re bath mat. It had taken him to Mars, planet of free Mars bars, then betrayed him by thrusting him in vat of boiling chocolate and threatening to pull Horace's whiskers out. Parents as usual sleep through Benjy's howls with devastating indifference. Took him to check Horace's whiskers. Had to count them twice, infuriating sleeping Horace who bit Benjy in revenge, thus increasing Betrayal Factor and size of tidal wave pouring over moi *from direction of Ickle Bro's peepers.*

Tucked him up in bed. Turned out lights. Turned off Father's komputer. He was sprawled asleep in front of it at crucial moment in CITYSCAPE. Knocked half-empty lager can into Only Father's lap by accident. He merely groped damp trouser region smiling and muttering 'time, gentlemen, please', clearly a throwback to earlier era of sensible licensing laws.

Returned to bed pondering Byooty Sleep, Nachur of Yuniverse, hairdo of Adam Stone, identity of Navel Gurl in Library Etck. Asleep at dawn.

Must comfort self with prospect of this Alphabet creating zillions of sales worldwide. I begin, as before, with the AAAAAAze . . .

ABSEILING

A-A-Aaaaaaaaaaaaaaaaaaaaaaaaaaa . . .

If you think El Chubb is ever going to be seen dead Abseiling you have an *autre* think coming, *mon amie*, and anyway if she were to pursue this seriously Luny activity dead is what she undoubtedly would be, and serve her right too. Why, I ask you, dear Student of LettyLIFE, did the great Creator of the Werld, the Yuniverse Etck invent gravity and bad eyesight to keep us stuck on the surface of the planet and imagining the globe is nice and flat if all we do is swing about in the air instead? Outward bound types may find it sweeps cobwebs Etck from Slough of Despond. Personally, I think if this happens it's only because Abseiling makes you realize there are more frightening things in LIFE than Spots, Flat Chests, Mad Parents Etck, to whit, staring Banana in the face while swinging on the end of a piece of string. Abseiling Lunies allegedly stave off this Certain Fate by investing in lots of safety harnesses, helmets, padding, LIFE insurance (not really) Etck.

27

ABYSS

The Pit of Despond into which you fall when your
LIFE Plans backfire, eg: Lurve Object telephones
three minutes late, Gerbil shreds only pair of
leggings, Wig falls out after bleaching, Etck. This
first is worst and is the longest three minutes known
to Yumanity, but is better than your Lurve Object
never phoning at all, as happens to *moi*.

See also DEPRESSION, FEELINGS,
PSYCHIATRISTS.

ADVERTISING

Adored Mother and Father sometimes go on as if
Advertising only started having its Wicked Way
with us all from about the 1960s, when window-
cleaners-turned-fashion-photographers started
manipulating our Dreamz with pix of Gurlz-Next-
Door who happened to look like Supermodels, and
sneaky psychology began to replace the old corny
stuff of actors looking like ventriloquists' dummies
holding up products that nobody in their right
minds would believe in.

But I have seen in Old Bukes that Advertising
has used all manner of scams to make you believe
LIFE is meaningless without some vital Stuff or
other *for decades*. In the 19th century, conmen in top
hats were always getting people to believe they had

the Elixir of LIFE in a bottle. After all, it only takes
advantage of a Yuman quality that Yr Favourite
Tomes, namely those by El Chubb, is always on
about – ie: WORRYING. Biggest Worry of all, of
course, is Banana. Advertisers don't quite tell you
they can get rid of that, but they do say they can
make Yr LIFE so wonderful in the meantime that

when you do finally get there, you will Know that you lived LIFE to the full, thanks to Gluggo Drain Cleaner Etck.

Advertisers defend their often dodgy practices, bending of The Truth Etck by saying it makes people buy more and therefore creates jobs, stimulates Economy Etck. I reckon the only Good Thing to be said about Advertising is that if you get to work in it yrself they pay Qu. Good Dosh. Then, of course, *you* have to learn all those speeches about how it creates Jobz, stimulates Etck Etck . . .

ALADDIN

Many a time I have burnt midnight oil in attempts to make lamp that will grant everyone all of their LIFE's wishes — ideas on a postcard please. I wld certainly like to have a genie I cld call up at any time of the day or night, who would make my every wish Come True. (Unfortunately I think even if you have a V. Handsome Genie you are not allowed to get it to fulfil Yr Every Wish personally, as it were, because it is of the Spirit Werld, shame, whinge Etck.) Sadly, the only genie I have met is my Mother's boss at the library, Jeanie Stropp, whose name doesn't enable her to do anything magical except send out fines to single parents on income support so fast they've hardly had time to get the books home in the first place. Maybe this is how Aladdin's genie got his original treasure together.

ALPHABET

Why not make one for your little sibling? Or for your worst enemy? A is for Agony, B is for Blisters, C is for Cyanide, D is for Dume, E is for Ennui . . .

ANIMALS

If you don't want eggs from battery hens, check they are 'free Range'

Many Teenage Worriers are concerned about Animal Rights and certainly if you look at how chickens Etck are treated in today's hi-tech farms you feel V. Sick. It is hard to imagine that the Food-chain, delicate balance of Nachur Etck is not being seriously disturbed by the imprisoning, injecting and dodgy feeding of our Animals and since campaigning for their right to a decent LIFE also makes us have a better chance of same, it seems a V.

Sane thing to L. Chubb. It is well worth finding out more about this and joining an ecological group as there is V. Little you can do about Animal Rights on your own.

Respecting your pet(s) is one thing you *can* do and, as someone with allergy to cats who still has one on her bed most nights, I know what I'm talking about. NB If you *are* allergic, though, don't get a pet. My folks would not have got me Rover if they had known. It really isn't V. Good for you. Remember the old saying: 'A pet is not just for Christmas, it is for LIFE.' And certainly that cute ickle ball of wool may not seem such fun when it is a vast panting hound demanding walkies every two hours and half a cow for breakfast. THINK B4 you get a pet, whether you really want to look after it, rain or shine. If you DO, it will reward you with Lurve.

See CATS, DOGS, GERBILS, HORSES, PETS

ANTHROPOLOGY

This is a V. Fantastic thing for Teenage Worriers to study as it helps you understand Nachur of Yumanity. Why do we need lightbulbs, toothpaste, fishcakes Etck when we could be communing with Grate Unknown from Hammock Etck? It takes you away from yr own obsessions with spots Etck and on to a wider canvas which shows you that it's possible to be unhappy (I mean happy) in a thousand different ways.

Imagine, for a moment, the incredibly different LIVES led in Four Corners of Globe by other kinds of people: nomads like the Bedouin, who still travel by camel and are respected not for possessions, but for 'Reputation', ie: nice attributes like honesty, kindness Etck which our society seems to undervalue in El Chubb's humble opinion. Or how about the Wayapi, the Amazonian People who have been hunting in the Amazon Forests for 5 centuries?

Then there are Aborigines, right on the doorstep of White European culture, who are the indignant (I mean indigenous) peoples of Australia. When I was best frendz with Sarah Spiggott before she took Daniel from me, she told me a lot about them and about how they, like the Native Americans before them, are being hounded off their lands and 'Westernized' Etck. Why anyone shld think people wld prefer to live in high-rise slabs of concrete rather than roaming deserts, mountains Etck with their mates is a mystery to *moi*.

A V.V. old Aboriginal artist, Emily Kngwarreye, who died in 1996, did not see any white people until she was 9 years old. She started painting in her 70s and became V. Rich and Famous, exhibited all over the werld and earnt vast amounts of dosh but continued to live in traditional hut. Maybe there is a LIFE lesson here . . .

APOLOGIES

One of the scariest things I ever heard is that the first French word that Hitler's troops learnt when they were invading France was '*Pardon*', which is French for 'Sorry'. This is an instance of how the spirit of the Apology can be abused, but unfortunately there are many much less serious but still disturbing egs than that of how people say 'sorry' as a habit when they don't really mean any such thing. Those big, shambling blokes who look like yaks and push you out of the way to get on the

You can take apologies too far...

bus sometimes say it (if they notice you're there at all); so do V. Busy Looking people with suits and mobile phones who crash into you and say it having realized only that something soft and squeaking might have scratched their polished elk-skin briefcase in the course of hurtling off it into the path of a speeding truck.

It is clear, however, that if you hope to avoid some of LIFE's pitfalls then it is a good idea to know how to Apologize gracefully, and that an Apology genuinely offered is one of the most attractive and disarming qualities a person can have. Actions, however, have to be more important than werds, or Apologies are nothing more than luke-warm air.

36

APPEARANCES

Do not judge by Appearances, you can't tell a buke
by its cover, handsome is as handsome does Etck.
Sadly, these fine phrases are not V. Comforting to
your average puny, speckly, suppurating Teenage
Worrier. Of course I wld *like* to subscribe to the
Belief that the Soul Shines through even the
cloudiest exterior and that I am Lurved for myself
alone and not for mere Outward Appearances . . .

  I blame the Teen Magazines like *Tru Luv*, *Smirk*,
Yoo-Hoo! and the new, best-selling, excruciating
Peteet for making us Gurlz wish we were spindly
giantesses with floorless complexions, eyes like
planets and teeth like a double row of keyboards.
And now we're supposed to bake our own bread, run
for parliament and have a couple of designer kiddies
too.

  Smirk would say: 'Find a style that suits you and
stick to it.' The next week the same writer would
tell you to 'Experiment with a wide variety of styles,

don't be shy.' With advice like this, no wonder
Teenage Worriers are confused.

L. Chubb would say, 'Don't concentrate on your
weak points. If you don't mention them, no-one else
will notice.' eg: A V. Nice gurl at school told me
how miserable her nose made her recently and ever
since it has made me miserable too, as I can't stop
noticing it. I never did before.

CONFIDENCE TIP:

Banish pix of Naomi Campbell Etck from your
poster collection and instead go for V. Interesting
women like Virginia Woolf, Grandma Moses,
Roseanne Etck. This will have added value of
making you look V. Intelligent as well as, um, good
looking by comparison (not that we care what
people think, do we? cough, splutter).

See also FASHION, IMAGE.

ARCHITECTURE

HRH Prince Charles, Hair to the Throne (does his
bald patch mean his chances of becoming King are
diminishing further?), often goes on about how
terrible Architecture is today, how arrogantly
Architects design things that look like giant
cheesegraters, milk bottles Etck for people to live
and work in, without caring about the nice old
crumbling, pigeon-infested buildings standing
around them.

El Chubb, Heroine of 21st Century City Renewal
Etck and killer *CITYSCAPE* champione, wld qu.
like to consider Architecture as a poss. career if the
impossible happens and Hollywood stardom does
not pan out. It seems to *moi* that it is a role in LIFE
that can considerably cheer up the Yuman Race as
they go about their daily grind, and Better Housing
in particular is something that wld help lift the
mood of many people currently inhabiting V.
Depressing places built out of slabs of stained
concrete Etck.

But it is not just a matter of the right Architects,
but the right Attitude too. A few V. Flash
Architects can get stacks of dosh for buildings
hardly anybody uses, while councils Etck have to
build estates on budgets which mean the tenants
practically have to make their own bricks. There is
something Wrong here surely, and if you care about
this Ishoo, you cld:

a) Study to become an Architect yrself and try to
help.

b) Submit proposals to the Teenage Think Tank
for renewal of Urban Living Etck.

ART

Art is usually thought of as a V. Posh thing that yr
parents Etck pretend to be interested in,

celebrations of the highest manifestations of the Yuman Spirit Etck, but for this reason Art that is being made by new Artists sometimes isn't recognized as Art at all. Some Artists today try to undermine V. Respectable Art by making sculptures out of wet T-shirts with oranges inside, dead fish, or lavatory bowls exhibited in posh galleries Etck. I must say I sympathize with this Attitude, and so does Benjy, who prob enjoys this kind of Art more than any other.

Graffiti

NEWTON'S LAW OF GRAFFITI: "What goes up, stays 'up'"

Thanks to the indelible Paint Co.

El Chubb nevertheless recommends escaping LIFE's trauma by immersing self in Art as often as poss, appreciating great pix Etck. It is not a matter of just going 'wow, wicked' Etck at Posh Art you have been told it's OK to like even though you don't understand why, but of twigging how some of the cleverest people at recreating LIFE on canvas, in bukes Etck, saw Lurve, Hate, War, Peace, Washing-Up, Plukes Etck, hundreds of years ago. It can be V. Humbling and Enlightening because it helps you to realize people have felt just like you lots of times before.

See also HOBBIES.

ASSERTIVENESS TRAINING

V. Imp to be Assertive in today's Cut-and-Cut Werld where the haves have lots and the have-nots have not. But take it easy: first, learn to spell werd 'boo', then gently practise it in front of mirror before trying it out on new-hatched chicks, progressing through sparrows, pigeons and ducks before graduating to full-blown goose.

ATTITUDE

Having the Right Attitude is thought by Adults to mean being V. Eager, perlite Etck. Certainly, behaving decently to fellow folk helps a lot in LIFE but in Koolspeak having lots of Attitude means, well, being Kool.

See also POSING.

CHAPTER TWO
BBBBBBBBBze

Father in deep depression having got to final stage (he says) of CITYSCAPE *only to find I'd turned it off without saving game, thus blowing weeks of painstaking research. Mother making pointed remarks to effect he could spend time researching novel or else writing for the* Slob *instead of the worthy papers he contributes to now, and therefore make a few quid Etck. Father's furious response to this interference somewhat stilled by Only Mother's crool observation that he now seems to have let himself go to extent of weeing himself whilst in drunken stupor. Kept quiet about lager bottle mishap Etck. Feel badly about this, however — may confess when Feeling Stronger or Only Mother about to evict Only Father Etc.*

My attempts with purple dye to assuage Benjy's fears re bath mat resulted in large indigo blobs all over bathroom walls and rest of floor (cork tiles). Bath mat itself remains resolutely puce. Benjy now convinced alien mat has been sick in bathroom. Mother insists I spend paltry savings on paint to repair damage (bang goes new navel-revealing outfit for film course).

Tonight is first night of the course. Sick with Worry re lack of knowledge of subject, nothing to wear Etck Etck. Aggy is coming back from skule with me to calm savage breast, help decide on wardrobe Etck.

Got back to find Father and Benjy both still in tears,

Benjy refusing to go near bathroom at all until mat removed and Martian vomit cleared up. Mother insists I cannot go out until bathroom shinier than rap star's skull Etck. After half an hour of scrubbing, Aggy (oh Noble frend in need!) offered to finish on her own so I could go to New Directions. *How will I ever repay her?*

Arrive, V. Flustered, at vast municipal building resembling DSS office (shortly to be sold to grasping Capitalist thugs thus depriving us of Welfare State Etck). Ask man at door where to go. His response V. Rude. Baffled, but see below for explanation of Strange Behaviour.

Wend way tragickly through network of peeling corridors, stairs, lifts, dead ends Etck and finally come upon dazzling logo: NEW DIRECTIONS START HERE. *Nearly turn back but realize I will be laughing stock among Aggy and family if I return empty-headed, so nervously enter, V. Late. All eyes swivel to regard* moi *– strange creature-from-other-werld whose outfit (Kool black sweatshirt available from El Chubb Enterprises) is embroidered with honest but unappealing sweat-stains and purple foam. Realize face may be in similar condition and have time only to register gleaming wooden floor, gleaming glare of tutor and four of the swivelling eyes – the deep dark soulful gaze of Adam Stone and the shallow dark haughty stare of Ms Navel from the library. Arg.*

Squeeze myself in beside a comforting-looking older woman of about 40, who rustles strangely as I brush past, and a V. Interllekshual looking needle of a cove who is furiously scribbling in a vast notebook which looks as if it might suddenly snap shut and eat him, like Venus Flytrap.

The lecturer introduces himself (for the second time, he mentions, glancing pointedly at moi*) as Phil Sleeve MA B.Phil. RSC.*

He'll talk, he says with grim satisfaction, for most of this evening. Practical werk next week. Hopes there won't be any more latecomers (glares at moi*).*

Then, in V. Toady Tones, he simpers that it is his delight to have the privilege of welcoming Candice Carthage from the Los Angeles Film School . . . daughter of most famous Hollywood director and already such a distinguished student in her own right . . . has won prize with first film at numerous festivals, an extraordinary achievement for one so young . . . great honour her father thought this Humble Course suitable for her Etck Etck.

Candice (you guessed who she is) allows a roseate flush to suffuse her damask mug. Lowering her forest of lashes to sweep her carefully sculpted cheek and winking (I swear it*) at Adam Stone, she murmurs modestly that it is only one of many courses she is sampling for her thesis, adding graciously that she is certain it will be among the most enthralling.*

Candice... lowering her forest of lashes...

45

An awestruck hush.

*Is this really the daughter of Mogul Mogul Junior the
Third? Hollywood Leg End? Maker of* Mission
Interminable, Relatives of the Lost Clerk, Raiders of
the Lost Armband, Erratic Quark *and the soon to be
released* Anville*?*

*Adam Stone strains forward, his eyes twin oceans of
desire. Tutor wriggles playfully and for next half-hour
addresses all his remarks to Candice's navel.*

*He will begin with a brief, he hopes (sickening wink at
Candice), survey of the reasons we are all here, although
he must apologize for going over old ground in the case of
some advanced students (grovelling smirk at Candice), he
is sure that even the most brilliant of men – and women
(more oozing in Candice's direction) – had to start at, for
want of a better werd, the beginning (nervous giggle,
clearing of throat, wagging of tail Etck). And where better
to start than a child's first experience of the Silver Screen?
. . . blah . . . blah . . .*

*I am just sobbing self to sleep in back row when I am
roused by a name . . . what is the loathsome lecturer
saying?*

*'. . . perhaps best encapsulated in the glorious but
tragickly undervalued children's classic, the story of the
10-year-old girl on a remote, windswept Highland
Island . . .'*

*Am I hearing things? Is he intoning a passage from the
book I got out of the library? Surely not? But, yes!*

*My moment of redemption is near. Mr Sleeve may not
impress me, but it is my duty to impress him – and, by so*

doing, win Adam Stone's admiration from the clutches of Candice Carthage. Hyperventilating, I gasp in reedy tones: 'Yes, and isn't it wonderful when the salt of the popcorn bursts like a sunrise in her mouth and the cinema darkens and . . .'

'Goodness!' exclaims Mr Sleeve.

I am aware of three pairs of eyes sweeping in my direction; the dark waves of Stone, the penetrating Carthage beam, the rheumy gaze of Sleeve.

They are impressed.

'You have read the book?' Sleeve glances at his register.

'Scarlett, I see – obviously from a family of cinema lovers. Of a sort, at any rate.'

To a flurry of sniggers, but without missing a beat, Sleeve drones to a conclusion.

My misery at being named after the heroine of Gone with the Wind has never scaled a more exquisite moment of glume. My only mission at this point is to get out of there in manner that makes Sonic the Hedgehog look like Droopy Etck. But although the voice of Granny Chubb, never far from my thoughts, whispers 'more haste, less speed', it is too late. Cannonball Chubb has collided with her neighbour, the stout, motherly figure festooned with carrier bags, which turn out to carry cameras, lenses, zooms, projectors and every other cinematographic device known to moviedom, now skidding hazardously across suicidally polished wooden floor. Speculate on legging it, but blurt apologies and stoop to scoop up what I know to be the unsaveable remains of priceless camera.

There is a blinding flash of light. Darkness descends.

Dear Reader, has Yr Hopeless Heroine fainted in despair, to be revived by the soft breath of Adam Stone upon her brow, and other vital bits? No such luck. She has tripped over a lighting cable and fused the building. By the time Mr Sleeve had enjoyed calming everybody down (especially Candice) and performed man-of-the-people routine on grumbling janitor carrying torch, Mrs Stout had retrieved most of her hardware (all miraculously undamaged, being made of pre-Planned Obsolescence materials) and exited cheerfully announcing that she had come to wrong class and was looking for place to photograph nude male models. (At this point another blinding flash, this time inside my apology for a brain, as I realize a double-entendre *in the course title. The man at the door as I came in must have thought I was asking the way to* Nude Erections . . .)

Exit of Mrs Stout and WW2-style blackout drama united the class in cheerful camaraderie while we all jotted down what we were supposed to bring in next week (for form's sake, as I knew I would not be coming back, I borrowed Mr Needle's biro and wrote it on the back of my hand, where it mingled with the purple dye rather attractively).

I felt I could now slither out, never to return, when I felt a hand on my shoulder. I turned to gaze into the eyes (glowing orbs Etck) of Adam Stone.

'Is this yours?'

'No! . . . um, yes.'

How could I deny that the plastic bottle, whose purple trail led across the otherwise gleaming floor, up my stone-

*washed denim legs and into my pocket, was in fact my
bottle of dye? 'Oh, silly me. It's my baby brother.'*

'Looks like Indigo Dream *to me.' And he flashed a
smile of such radiance that my heart flew to entwine with
his for eternity and we got married that evening. Whoops.*

*In fact, he said, 'Cheerio then, see you next week. Let's
hope Sleeve doesn't roll up for the practical.' He winked. I
think. And disappeared into the dusk, a vision of long-
limbed grace with undulating Beumb to match Etck.*

*I floated home on his wink and practised rolling up T-
shirt to reveal navel, but on contemplating grey gritty bits
embedded therein decided to pursue own course to Erotic
Charisma rather than borrow methods of Lesser Mortals
Etck. Found sparkling bathroom, sleeping and placated
Benjy, adoring Rover and cheese sandwich with crusts cut
off left out by Only Mother. Little thingz mean a lot.*

*I'm writing this V.V.V. Late at night, trying to make
sense of my tangled emotions. 'See you next week, see you
next week.' And that witty little throwaway thing about
Sleeve, who he obviously didn't like. Maybe then he wasn't
gazing adoringly at Candice Carthage??? But was that
really a wink or did he have a fly in his eye?*

Maybe I should go next week?

*If so, must think of some witty pun about Sleeve to
impress Adam. Drift into jumbled dreamland musing
along these lines . . . 'For such a short Sleeve he certainly
goes on too long . . . makes you want to give him a* cuff
*. . . glad you're in a sleeveless vest, wish I cld say the same
for the course . . .' Etck.*

Arg.

BALLET

In my Darling Mother's childhood there were supposed to be two types of Gurl – the ones who liked Ballet and the ones who liked horses.

This seems still true today and there are plenty of Teenage Worriers whose main LIFE Dream is still to twirl about pointily in tulle, and if you don't know what tulle is then you probably like horses.

My own experience of Ballet was miserable, however: my V. Rich and V. Stingy Grandma Gosling forked out for me to have Ballet lessons when I was 7. My Father took a video of the Ballet class Christmas show the year I was 9, and it definitely proves that a hippo really can be crossed with a giraffe, whatever David Attenborough might say.

Despite the Ballet Mistress's determined attempts to plonk me right at the back and give me the absolute minimum to do, I stick out like sore thumb of ogre on hand of elfin. My stifled sobs can be heard on the sound track. Two years of misery ended when this film was shown to Grandma Gosling, who immediately withdrew the funds. The relief was enormous, but I have a small pair of pink satin ballet shoes wrapped in tissue paper under the debris of my clothes cupboard and one day – who knows? – some fawn-like descendant of my Union with Adam may step into them and dance on air . . .

See also DANCING.

I stick out like sore thumb of ogre on hand of elfin

NO KENNEL
10 puppies
to support

BEGGAR

I often think when I see Beggars sitting in doorways looking V. Pathetick and holding even more Pathetick dogs on bits of string

a) There but for Fate go *moi* and

b) People in the Govt shld try it for a week and see what they think.

There is big campaign in the Media to convince you Beggars all have Rolls-Royces parked round the corner, houses with gravel drives in Essex Etck, but personally I do not believe this, and anyway the Enterprise Culchur which helped create so many Beggars is only based on selling people just about anything for as much dosh as you can, so why not sell people the idea that you're a starving homeless wretch?

When I am PM I will bring in a law that says everyone, wherever you come from, has to do a week's begging, like my Adored Father sez National Service used to be years ago.

Then

a) Begging wld not seem so threatening to fine upstanding citizens worried about Crime Wave, Moral Collapse Etck and

b) Everyone wld get a chance to see how other half lives, which might do some thingz to them they wld remember for LIFE.

BOTTOMS

Let us have a last look (sigh) at men's Bottoms, before they all have to start wearing dresses. You

Boyz in Frocks Pt 2
Designs by
Armani-Westwood-Chubb

may doubt this, but it cld become V. Imp for Future of Yumanity, as lowered sperm count brought on, among other things, by the wearing of tight jeans threatens species Etck, although as far as I know the movement for men to wear frocks is still only limited to sections of the Gay Community. I think it cld catch on quite fast if Armani or someone went with it. I wouldn't mind seeing Adam in a scarlet chiffon sheath (writhe, phew) and since everyone seems to agree the future is female (I read somewhere that 80% of the jobs created in the next 10 years will go to Gurlz, who will then make up 44% of all professionals) I guess it's time for Boyz to be more like Gurlz rather than striving for us Gurlz to be more like them and make more bombs Etck.

New El Chubb slogan: 'BEUMBS NOT BOMBS!'

BROTHERS

Sibling rivalry
starts young...

Picture of innocence →

Benjy thinking floor has turned into Loch Ness

I have mixed feelings about brothers. I have one big brother, Ashley, who is Perfect In Every Way, and a little one who is frightened of floors. Between an Angel and a Luny, what chance does a normal average Teenage Worrier have?

NB Teenage Worriers with sisters have same probs, joyz Etck as far as I can see, except they borrow yr clothes more if you are a gurl. Er, on the whole.

BULLIES

Teenage Worriers and skulekids often think that
Bullies are only people who kick yr ball over the
fence (poss plural in the case of Male Teenage
Worrier, ha), tear yr bukes, turn skule into
Blackboard Jungle Etck. But there are Bullies
everywhere in LIFE because it is about making yrself
feel strong by hurting someone you think is weaker,
and meant to be a sign that you are hurt yrself but
don't want anyone to know. In my skule they say
'don't bully the bully', ie, to whit: if you victimize
the Bully to get them to stop they just get worse
because it confirms their inner sense of how horrible
they are anyway. I am often V. Sympathetick to this
explanation. I am often also tempted to find an ex-
member of the SAS thrown on scrap heap by Govt
Cuts Etck, and get him to brush up on his
undercover interrogation methods on some of the
Bullies I know. This is a Base Emotion To Be
Resisted, but is also something that happens. NB It

<u>Victim</u>   <u>Bully</u>

N.B. Appearances can be misleading

is *V.V. Important*, if you ARE bullied, to report it to
your mum, dad, teacher Etck. Keep on about it
until they do something, which should be soon.

BUSKERS

Who brighten up the streets and tubes in Inner
Cities with their cheery renditions of V. Old pop
songs Etck, and are consequently moved on and
abused by officious fok who would presumably
rather they just lived in cardboard boxes drinking
meths or maybe entertaining their fellow inmates as
members of the prison population, which at the rate
thingz are going will soon be just about all of us.
(Thinks: this is obviously the Master Plan. The Govt
intends to put everybody in prison except
themselves and their mates, treat all werk as
donated free to help prisoners learn to be decent
citizens, thus increasing their earnings by 80
zillion %.)

When you are 18 you are officially allowed to
busk (apart from getting moved on Etck, as above). I
think it is worth all Teenage Worriers considering
Busking as a career to help pay fees through Art
School, University, Drama College Etck, which the
Govt used to pay for in the Golden Olden Daze
when our parents were but striplings Etck. In
London's seething Covent Garden, frinstance, there's
a bloke who jumps over matchboxes. This can't be
that hard to learn, surely?

Busker Tips

NB. Only if You're 18+

1. Get a **SKILL** - cld be just spraying self gold and pretending to be Statue of Liberty ← (not OK re-allergies as convulsive sneezing diminishes Stately Effect).

2. Get a **PITCH**. Check bye-laws to avoid fines.

3. **BULLY** the **AUDIENCE** (nicely)

   e.g: "After the count of TEN I want to hear how LOUD you can cheer 1, 2, 3... 10 (puny shout) - a beautiful talented bunch like you can do MUCH better". Soon audience will cheer V. Loud which attracts more people. **THEN** you remind them this is your **LIVING**. "I could," you fib, "be playing West End Theatres, but I CHOOSE the streets, to have RAPPORT with my audience (or audient....) but I need JUST enough to keep me and my pet alive".

4. Get a **PET**. Cute but **skinny** (worm, stick insect). Not really. Pets need RESPECK. See ANIMALS.

5. Get the **DOSH** "So I don't want

anything from you, except what you can afford. Put your hand in your pocket After the Show and give me what you think I'm WORTH. No MORE. Take your money out of your pocket, FOLD it" (Laughter) "No, honest, ONE Pound is enough".

6. Do Your ACT. Make it look really HARD. Like the bloke who gets off a straight jacket in 2 mins when he could do it in 30secs.

7. Pass round HAT. If you have done act V. Badly you will get old socks, bus tickets Etck. If well, the Werld could be yr. oyster.

L. Chubb's Audience. (But just WAIT till I'm 18).

CHAPTER THREE
CCCCCCEEEEEze

11 phone calls later – 7 to Aggy, 4 to Hazel – a few consultations with packs of cards, lucky rabbit's foot, God Etck later . . . I have decided to be independent minded, throw caution to the winds, toss my bonnet over the windmill and attend next week's film lesson. What have I got to lose? Only my pride (er, self-esteem, sense of worth, notion of Meaning in Void Etck. Gulp).

Must admit other factor was Hazel's V.V.V.V. Kind offer to lend me her video camera to help with my project on Urban Dekay. All I have to do is pay for half an hour's worth of tape. She is going to let me have it for two weeks!! Sometimes, I reflect sadly, it is V. Nice to have the odd frend with dosh . . .

Spend whole of Saturday combing flea markets for clothes and combing fleas out of Rover in attempt to raise self-respect. Wish I could follow my own excellent advice to stick to something V. Simple, but desire to cover up strange twigs and branches that sprout randomly as apologies for limbs from scrawny trunk of Yrs Truely is overwhelming me.

Luckily on third trip to market am made to see sense by loyal Aggy (if only she had equal sense about her own dear form and would throw away those lime-green culottes) and finally choose V. Understated T-shirt in Ebony with just the merest hint of Jet and some slinky trousers the colour of fog, with a faint luminous sheen. V. Pleased, despite guilt-pangs re spending hard-saved dosh on self, instead of GCSEs (Granny Chubb's Specs Endeavour).

Home with long-suffering Aggy to try various styles for wig. After three hours of coiling and plaiting we decide dreadlocks do not suit blotchy Chubb complexion so Aggy gets out iron and irons each corkscrew straight. As she pulls last strand of wig into agonizing scorching tautness, I am aware of large drops of water plopping onto ironing board.

Has my Only Mother invested in a steam iron? Has Only Father been fixing plumbing again? No, the drops of water are the tears of dear Aggy, who is remembering how her mother used to iron her frizzy mop when she was 10, in the halcyon days before she ran off with the postman.

Poor Aggy, lumbered with tearful, though caring father and so many siblings I can never remember all their names . . . Do I care only for myself? Am I the person who vowed to devote LIFE to Nunnery, Art Etck and forsake Sins of Flesh? Spend next three minutes comforting Aggy and offer to make her cheese sandwich. Sadly, no cheese or bread in house but she tearfully accepts half a digestive biscuit before going home to cook for the small village that resides in her father's two-bedroom flat.

Resolve to divert some of earnings as film director into improving Aggy's lot before plunging through my old portfolio of photographs in order to find a selection worthy of taking to the film course. Need Angle that might werk up into Project. Sleeve has requested that we bring a

*storyboard of ideas along and he will choose the best three
for us all to collaborate on. I decide that Urban
Deprivation is burning issue and that pics of Granny
Chubb eating tin of cat food (or possibly cat, though Rover
may need fee in excess of Tom Cruiser earnings to pose for
same), tramp with dog on string and V. Harrowing pic of
Aggy taking 4 little siblings to skule on misty morning
will form basis of Grate Werk.*

*Jot down few ideas re gap between Rich and Poor ever-
widening (worst in Western Werld, according to posh
newspaper written by caring interllekshuals who shake
heads over areas like mine from windows of Volvo estates)
and fall into bed convinced of future fame, fortune Etck.*

CAFFEINE

It always surprises me how parents let their little
diddums kiddies eat all kinds of junk they wouldn't
dream of feeding to their pets, viz: 'Don't you dare
give Fido a chocolate biscuit, you know it'll make
his coat dull, his nose dry, he'll get hyperactive and
stay out all night at Raves Etck.'

But while Fido, Puss and the goldfish are fed
with stringent rigour, little Darren and Karen are
stuffed with Caffeine, fizz and sugar, starch and
bubbles. They zoom into acned adolescence at a
serious dietary disadvantage in the humble opinion
of El Chubb, Dietary Adviser to Divorced Members
of Royal Family Etck.

On *le autre main* you get loads of kids who have eaten nought but bread you need a fork-lift truck to carry, lentils, rice Etck until they turn into yuman beanbags (even at *parties*, where the 'sweeties' are sultanas, grue, yeech, puke Etck), who are frequently weedier, spottier, paler and infinitely more glumey than their mates.

'It's all a question of balance,' as my dear old Primary Skule Teacher, Miss Scales (how I miss her), used to say.

Caffeine is also unique in ye Drug Culchur (along with tannin, which is what's also in tea, and coats yr insides with something like boot polish if Granny Chubb's teapot is anything to go by) for being socially acceptable, even at church fêtes. Suppose Conservative Ladies called their fund-raising

gatherings 'Caffeine Mornings'? What wld happen
to attendance?

'A nice fix of tannin, Vicar?'

Wheel on the soft drugs trolley and LIVE!

See DIETS for El Chubb's perfectly balanced
nutrition guide for today's Yoof.

CAMPAIGN

'Campaign' has several meanings – there are
Campaigns in wars, when muddy, cursing V.
Unhappy Boyz with guns spend months, or maybe
years, trying to win back one molehill with a V.
Baffled looking mole standing on it off the other
side and call it a Glorious Victory, Turning Point in
History Etck. There are also Election Campaigns,
which are also about trying to win said molehill off
the other side, but without guns (usually). But the
kind of Campaigning most interesting for Teenage
Worriers is where you choose something you are V.
Passionate About (preferably The Environment, The
Beumb, The Planet, Animal Rights Etck rather than
Brad Pittbull) and try to Get Something Done
About It.

Why do this? I hear you cry, in breathless
anticipation . . . because

a) It may be good for the Yuman Race, future
generations Etck

b) It is a way of DOING rather than
WORRYING.

CAREER

As you know, dearest reader, I am V. Lucky in already having chosen my career as werld famous film director, but what to do after skule is V. Big Worry for many.

A Career used to mean doing the same job for LIFE, with a bit of luck getting better paid at it until they give you a gold-plated Zimmer frame. Now it means just staying on yr feet however many times they pull the rug out from under you. In which respeck, it seems to me the word Career has now come closer to its other meaning, as in 'careering toward the precipice' Etck.

El Chubb's advice for the 90s is: make the most of Yoof while you have it, learning anything that might turn out to be useful later, and staying at skule as long as poss. Since there is no such thing as olde-fashioned job security, you will need to re-invent yourself every few years anyway, so it is a V. Good Idea to learn one thing: HOW TO THINK.

Werld Leaders Etck find this task V. Difficult.

It is V. Imp to remember the famous saying of Eric Cantona – sorry, René Descartes: 'I think, therefore I am', or *cogito ergo sum* in Latin. It is closely related to the famous philosopher El Chubb's theory *agito ergo sum* or 'I Worry, therefore I am'. Descartes thought this up about 350 years ago, and apart from the fact that it might cause a few politicians and pop groups a few moments of doubt that they actually exist, it probably doesn't seem that much of a big deal to the rest of us these days.

Anyway, back to Careers. Careers Advisers at skule will be V. Helpful in telling you what you need to study to go in your desired direction Etck but it cld be worth finding out what the job prospects are at the end and nothing beats personal experience. So, if you want to be a Marine Biologist, try and MEET some of them and find out what the job is really like, and I bet they don't all play the harmonica and teach whales basketball Etck either.

See also JOBS, WORK.

CAR-WASHING

This is a job often done by Yoof in search of a few pennies for the next handful of dried grape-pips for dinner Etck. People sometimes prefer younger Car-washers than Teenage Worriers, unfairly suspecting the latter of using it as a cover to steal the radio Etck, but then regret this decision when two dripping Infants come to the door for their money while car looks as if it has been rallying in Outer Mongolia. Car-washing can be done at traffic lights, but this is not advisable, as people tend to drive off with you on the bonnet, threatening to start campaign in *Daily Wail* about you if you complain. Proper technique for Car-washing is: hose or splash car all over to shift grime, encourage it to dislodge with a soft brush, rinse off with clean water, then wipe dry with a clean chamois leather. You can intersperse into this activity

1) Hose down partner

2) Forget to close door whilst hurling bucket of water at car

We can learn from the younger generation

3) Miss car and hit passing escaped maniac instead Etck.

CATS

My Adored Father walled Rover up once. He was rewiring the house, a job that seemed to take about 10 years and through which we mostly sat in the dark with no telly, and took turns to do impressions from *EastEnders*, *Top of the Pops* Etck. Adored Father made a lot of unnecessarily large holes in cavity wall upstairs, Rover got in for a quiet snooze to escape from sound of Benjy thinking floor had turned into bird's nest soup, Adored Mother railing on about Medieval Living Conditions Etck; after various flashes, bangs, curses Etck Adored Father plastered up holes and suddenly we had the Cheshire Cat disappearing to leave only his grin, except that Rover disappeared to leave only her piteous whinge.

I mention this to draw yr attention to a famous feature of Cats, viz Curiosity. Cat lovers like *moi* do not like to contemplate the thought that Cats may do these things out of Stupidity rather than Curiosity, and I agree with the Egyptians, who made gods and goddesses out of Cats and did statues of them adopting V. Sensible flattering policy of making them look much taller and slimmer than they really are, a wise investment for a Good Deal in the After LIFE.

CELIBACY

Celibacy is Not Doing It. You wld not believe that anybody of legal age except Persons of God are in this position, or non-position, if you pay a lot of attention to the tabloid newspapers – or, for that matter, even the posh newspapers now, which are just as desperate to mention SEX whenever possible (unlike El Chubb, ahem).

Though the coverage of SEX in the papers, on telly Etck now makes it seem as if the whole nation is At It all day and all night, I don't believe it *moi*self. This is not just El Chubb rationalization at work. I just think people are beginning to find SEX much more interesting in the papers or on the Internet, or down the telephone than they do in Real LIFE. Perhaps this is the Safe SEX we hear so much about.

If you are Celibate as a Statement about Respeck, Waiting for Real Lurve Etck, then nobody thinks the worse of you and it can be helpful to ruminate on Spiritual rather than Carnal pleasures. V. Useful while still at skule, as thinking about SEX, Boyz Etck is wrecking my concentration.

CELLULITE

El Chubb never wants to hear this word again. But for those of you who missed the pix of Princess Di (which alleged that even *she* has it), it means fatty deposits around the thighs that make yr skin look dimply and blobby. No-one except an obscure handful of medics had heard of that thing that rhymes with smellubite until V. Recently when advertisers saw their chance to make fortunes by telling us all how to get rid of it. Even the photographer who took the photos of Princess Di didn't know what it was! His WIFE spotted it! This could be deemed an act of treachery to womankind, but I s'pose it was hard to resist the temptation to sell the photos for a fortune. El Chubb wld never be so corrupt with my tender moving photos of G. Chubb and Aggy Etck. At any rate, now we all DO know about it, even Teenage Worriers are Worrying about it! Grrrrr, rage, snarl.

CELLULITE FACTS:

All adult women and lots of Teenage Worriers have fat on their thighs. This is how it should be, and is part of Yuman adaptation to environment Etck.

Some look more dimply than others. So do some cheeks. So what? (I LIKE dimples.)

You can read every day in every daft magazine about creams, gels, leeches (not *really*, just checking you're concentrating), scrubs, rub-a-dub dubs Etck, all of which are V. Expensive and none of which work for more than about three seconds. Work on what, anyway? Do you really want a giant eraser to rub yrself out?

CENTAUR

Attractive beast, half-man, half-horse. Could this be
what we all want really?

Is this what we all want really?

CHESS

More interllekshual Teenage Lurvers might consider
giving Chess a break. It is not only played by
pointy-heads with hair like bursting mattress Etck,
but also by all of those who know that mental
proximity is as important as physical proximity and
anyway the one can lead to the other, or The Other,

72

as my Adored Father still unbelievably sez. After all, it has lots of Romantick Stuff in it, knights, castles, mating Etck. Unfortunately it also has pawns in it, but it was invented a long time ago, before European Court of Yuman Rights Etck, and one has to take it with pinch of salt since in many ways Chess otherwise resembles the evolution of Teenage LIFE, viz, to whit: cautious early moves backwards forwards and sideways Etck, deception about Real Intentions, eventual cornering of Lurve Object and inescapable conclusion of MATE. Sigh, swoon, Worry Etck . . .

CHRISTMAS

Alas and Woe for the passing of innocent childhood when all you wanted was a Fluorescent Pony with Wings and a Machine Gun with Rotating Bayonet Attachment. What you forget is that you never got the first because it was soppy and you never got the second because it was violent and all you got was krap like edukashunal jigsaws made of real wood where the pieces didn't fit. Not really – my parents weren't quite this barmy. But I must admit that, although Christmas isn't as exciting as it was when you propped your eyelids open to wait for the big bloke in the red suit (terrified you might REALLY see him), I still have deeply cosy feelings at this time of year.

OK, I like trees, tinsel, glitter, chortling robins Etck and enjoy cherubic face of Benjy as he hangs up stocking. Fact that cherubic face dissolves in tears V. Soon on realizing no Machine Gun with Bayonet Attachment, Lifesize Virtual Reality Football Pitch or Real Working Moon-Rocket emerges from stocking next morning does not diminish El Chubb's feeling of hopefulness at this time of year. Could be that it's 'cos everyone stops doing something else and you are allowed to wear V. Silly hats, slippers Etck and play komputer games for 10 hours without being nagged . . . (I mean go to Church, ponder on Life's Mystery, Spiritooality Etck).

CLASS SYSTEM

The Class System is V. Imp to LIFE in Britain, and people get V. Worried about it for the V. Good reason that it seems designed to make sure only one type of person (rich people) get the breaks and everyone else has to stay out of the ditch as best they can.

Long ago, Barons, Dukes, Earls Etck plundered the land and put up big signs over vast swathes of Ye Countryside saying 'MINE'. Their descendants built a lot of V. Pretty skules in green rural idylls, flash parts of town Etck, for their own children to go to, so they cld share tips about Plundering,

Exploiting, Pillaging, Shouting Etck. They also evolved V. Secret Code for addressing each other (*orffff*, ie: Off; *Gawlff*, ie: Golf; *Hice*, ie: House Etck) so they cld keep the best bits to themselves without Ye Peasants knowing where they were off to.

In the Class System there used to be three
groups – Upper Clarse, Middle Class and Werkin'
Class. This is now changing because most of the
hammering, bashing, digging, swearing Etck jobs
are now being done by robots and large parts of the
Werking Class aren't at werk, so the title seems a
bit daft. Also, the Upper Clarses have spent all their

Toffspeak for: 'He's gone into the house.'

Prolespeak for same

money on horses, paintings, Olde Retainers Etck, and have been forced to sell a lot of their best stuff to Lean, Hungry, Snapping Middle Classes On Way Up, so we may be moving to a new Class System which is just Middle Class and Underclass like in America. For *moi*self, I'm not certain which is better. These things are V. Complicated, and can make Yr Brain Hurt after a while.

CLUBS

Adored Mother and Father used to go to Klubs about a million years ago when they were young and carefree (cld such a thing be possible, I ask *moi*self?) and go on about how they heard Dire Straits in the days when they were all still skuleteachers or newsagents or something, standing as-close-as-I-am-to-you-now-and-Mark-had-a-strat-just-like-the-one-I-had-a-cardboard-replica-of Etck, yawn, cringe.

This seems to be exactly why they can't stand the Klubs Teenage Worriers go to today – it's all different now, you must all be raving mad, the places we went to were about music, not brain-scrambling noise, people behaved like Yuman Beans, cld have a quiet chat over a drink in a corner Etck. I know for a fact that Adored Father was banned from several Klubs in his locality as a Yoof, once for dancing so close to the stage he stuck his head through a loudspeaker, once for spitting at a bouncer in the mistaken impression that he was a famous punk star who would treat it as a cheery greeting.

But it's true that Klubs are different now, and though I'm too young to visit them (you've really got to be 18, or at least LOOK it, like pubs), the Klubbing werld has become as much a part of Yoof Culchur as pop bands, fanzines and clothes.

One of the V. Exciting things about Klubbing is that, like most really new developments in Pop, the inspiration for the best stuff came from the people who Do It, not a bunch of ex-hippies in white suits at a big record company. The danger now is that said record companies have realized how much money there is in Klubbing and are trying to take it all over and turn it into one massive Disco Disneywerld with everything interesting blanded out just the way they like it.

Parents like this better, of course, because they Worry that Klubland is full of Ecstasy-selling gangsters and can't wait for the day when the whole thing is organized like theme parks and there are franchises selling E-Burgers with ingredients approved by the Dept of Health, Virtual Reality DJs

← Veg 'E' burger
approved by
Dept. of Health

for the day when the Big Names are too expensive to bother to turn up in person any more, actors dressed as drug-dealers pretending to kill each other in the loos Etck. The balance between a risky werld created by Teenage Worriers so they both Have Fun and Worry in ways that aren't run by their parents or the Govt, and a werld in which you're no more likely to get killed or go mad than you wld be working the checkout in Sainsbury's is hard to get, but all the panicky stuff parents are told in the *Daily Wail* Etck certainly doesn't help.

Klubbing is mostly (I am told) about music and dancing and Having a Gd Time, and only a small bit about drugs, dume, glume Etck, the things that Teenage Worriers have to use their common sense about everywhere today, not just in the Toxic Rat. To keep up with what's going on (because it keeps changing every 5 minutes – Drum 'n' Bass, which does sound like being in a washing machine, but with a lot of knives and forks rattling around inside as well, is currently replacing House) it's a good idea to read the Klubbing magz, espesh the letters columns, which tell you a lot about how people just like you are feeling about this confusing scene. They're all V. Determined to stop the Klub scene falling into the hands of the Theme-Parkers and Disco-Multiplexers, and I only hope they can keep it up until El Chubb looks flash enough to lie to the bouncers about her age – some hopes Etck.

See MUSIC.

COMPUTERS

No Guide to LIFE wld be complete without considering Komputers because they have taken over many aspecs of our Lives, viz, to whit: there are many Boyz I wld say definitely prefer relationships with their Komputers to relationships with Gurlz, maybe it will only be a matter of time before they look like Pamela Anderson and as a matter of fact I don't think Pammy has so far given us any proof that she isn't a Komputer anyway, playing a V. Long Boring Game called *Boom & Bust*. Come to think of it, perhaps they cld make Komputers that look like Adam, with all necessary working parts including V. Super-developed (wait for it) Eternal Devotion programme networked to El Chubb @paradise.phew.steam.co.uk.

CONTRACEPTION

sadly, my detailed drawings of Teenage Worriers attempting to use condoms Etck. have been censored. But make sure you use one plus spermicide + diaphragm if poss if you have SEX. See SEX.

CHAPTER FOUR
DDDDDDze

Day 2 of film course
*Sick with Worry, saunter nonchalantly up steps, and
casually lope past Adam Stone, who luckily cannot hear (I
think) the herd of horses galloping beneath my breastbone.
Am just about to drop my portfolio casually at his feet —
and imagining his graceful bend to help me collect my
work, giving him an opportunity to gasp with admiration
at my heartfelt observations on Inner City deprivation —
when am pounced on by Mr Needle, demonstrating
priorities of A1 Nerdishness by demanding the return of
his biro.*

*Have naturally mislaid same and am forced to give him
my V. Nice pen (Only Father's actually, though he now
claims he can't write without a komputer, and due to
CITYSCAPE can't write with one, either), leaving me
with nothing to take notes.*

*During this encounter I spy out of the corner of my eye
that Candice is gliding up to Adam and engaging him in
intense, meaningful conversation using twin-barrelled
assault of mouth and navel simultaneously. Her top is also
cut both high and low at the same time, I am sorry to
report, and establishes that she has no need of a Wonder-
bra. Nachurally, all three of her secure a place next to
Adam.*

My misery is compounded by the following event.
Sleeve is looking through the portfolios.
He pauses, clearly amazed. 'Whose is this?'
'Mine,' I cry proudly, the horses once more fretting their
proud hooves in my gurlish breast.
'Fascinating,' he murmurs. Oh joy! He's going to
demonstrate the poetic, penetrating, profound, pulverizing
insights of the works of Yrs Truely to the class!
He shows them page after page.
Page after page.
It's Benjy's school work.
The life sickle of a tatpole.
Mi day at the zoooo.
Hou a plarnt wercks.
And so on.
And on.
I remember my Mother buying those identical portfolios
at her art class summer sale. But how could I have picked
up Benjy's?
'Were we thinking of cinéma naïf*? A new form?' asks*
the sadistic Sleeve. 'Or is your project purely domestic?'
I run from the room in confusion.
Even the noble Aggy is unable to comfort me.
Cry all night and next day I see Adam Stone at my
usual bus stop! He is talking to Candice Carthage.
Misery, glume, sackcloth, ashes. Hide behind hedge and
miss bus. Late for skule. Woe. Dume. Must throw self into
werk . . .

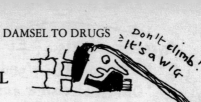

Don't climb!
It's a wig

Damsel

Damsels in Distress are s'posed to be V. Weedy
types holed up in towers waiting to let their hair
down to V. Nimble Laid-Back Princes who always
just happen to be walking in woods miles from
anywhere and hear the tragic cry of ye Damsel in
Distress, viz: 'Woe is me' Etck.

Alternatively Ye Damsels are sitting in castles
weaving webs of pure gold out of wire wool,
emptying oceans with sieves Etck until RESCUE. In
ye Olden Daze it might have been sensible for gurlz
to sit around waiting for someone to get them out of
a hole, but there should be no need to be a Damsel
in the 90s, and there aren't so many chances to be a
Damsel in Distress these days anyway, unless you
just stand around at the roadside in a short skirt in
hysterics because you don't know which end of yr
car the engine's in. My Adored Father always keeps
an eye open for this type of Damsel as he goes about
his benighted way, but he doesn't have much luck,
and El Chubb suspects this might be 'cos they're a
dying breed.

However, there are other kinds of Damsels in
Distress in the 90s: they just aren't the kind that
gets noticed by my Adored Father – or any other
adored (or unadored) father (or mothers, come to
that). Much as I wld like to say, if in distress, take
evasive action (like bopping wicked step-parent on
hooter and leaving home for wide welcoming world)

GREAT THOUGHTS of EL Chubb No. 128: Wonder if 'Damsel' came from 'Damn cell' as Rapunzel, Sleeping Beauty Etck. cursed their lonely towers, bowers, Etck....

things have not changed so much for Teenage Worriers as we would like to think. Many of us are still holed up with V. Overprotective parents or else are Not Cared About At All (which, believe me, is much worse). However, it *is* V. Imp not to expect some gorgeous BOY to appear and solve your probs (except in the case of *moi* and Adam) as if you have lots of probs, you are unlikely to be in the mood for Lurve anyway and the last thing that a 90s boy wants to do is support a family when he isn't ready to, especially his own.

DANCE

Gone are the daze, sighs my Hopeless romantick
Only Mother, when swave blokes in DJs swirled
elegant partners disguised as lampshades round
glistening parquet to string quartets Etck. They did
things like waltzes, fox-trots (always makes me
think of quadruped with the runs), polkas, gavottes
Etck and filled their dance cards like in those old
Jane Austen films (I mean, bukes, ahem). In fact,
this kind of Dancing went out of fashion when
Granny Chubb was a gurl and I don't believe my
Only Mother ever did it, although she seems to
think she might have, if she'd stayed in High
Society instead of dropping out with my dear Only
Father.

The only Old Dancing I Lurve and feel V. Jealous
of is Jive and I wish I could learn all that jumping
over heads and jitterbugging like in old Elvis
movies. Other OK trad types are Scottish, Country
and Tap as performed by V. Grate and Trooooly
Kool Stars like Fred Astaire, Ginger Rogers Etck.

What bugs *moi* a bit is it is V. Hard to know
exactly what to do when Dancing. I like to, er, go
with the beat Etck but unfortunately the beat
doesn't stay with *moi*. It could be that I'm just one
of those two-left-foot types who would have plonked
about in any period of Dance History, but I feel the
need of some help with this to stop lurking V.
Embarrassed in dark corners while everyone else lets

L. Chubb's Dance
(to tune of *Hokey Cokey*)
NB: Stage 4 is not possible for average human, but it's fun to try.
After stage 8, start again with right elbow, knees, hands, feet Etck

You put your LEFT Elbow OUT

1.

You put Your Left Elbow IN

2.

shake shake

You shake your head about

3.

And bang Your elbow on your CHIN

4.

— and that's what it's all ABOUT

it all hang out Etck. Slinky swinging of hips is best I have achieved so far.

See BALLET, CLUBS and MUSIC.

DAY-DREAMING

A day without Dreams is like a day without sunshine, sez *moi*. Can you imagine being unable to IMAGINE?

If you are a genuine Teenage Worrier, you will waste quite a lot of Day-dream time with Worrying

. . . ie: gazing nervously at yr spots and wondering
will they ever go, will anyone like you with them or
without them Etck. But Day-dreaming ends all this.
In it, you fantasize about doing all yr favourite
things with all yr favourite people.

ie: One of my Day-dreamz wld be lying in a bath
of warm liquid fudge with Adam and licking . . .
[CENSORED] . . . after which I wld win Pulitzer
Prize for fudge-wallowing and have werld at my
feet. That sort of thing. Quite modest. I have also
dreamed of the following:

89

Just some of my favourite daydreams. Others that I'd like –
to be a BOY (espech in changing rooms, heh heh)
or a famous detective

The QUALITY .....

PM INTRODUCES NEW LAWS TO FAVOUR YOUTH

Prime Minister Letty Chubb announced today that her government would declare
- **ZERO TOLERANCE** for poverty.
- **FREE** homes and travel passes for all.
- **Communal bikes and roller blades available at all tube and bus stations.**

Turn to page three to see L.Chubb's 20 point plan in full

But Day-dreaming can be quite low-key and free-associating. You can just gaze emptily into space and let your thoughts roam free. As long as you allow your thoughts to drift whimsically among the glades of fancy and invention (never plunging into Worry-land) you will wake from your Day-dream truely refreshed.

Lots of experiments have been done about the dangers of depriving people of Dreaming Sleep, but El Chubb's belief is that it is equally important to provide Dreaming Daze and that anyone bereft of opportunities for same will sink into glume. However, you have to use this information carefully. Parents, teachers Etck can become V. Grumpy when you say you are lying on the sofa in a week-old pair of socks watching *Neighbours* because it helps reconnect you with Yr Vital Subconscious Etck.

DEPRESSION

Glume, melancholy, long periods spent sobbing into pillow – all these are Part and Parcel of a Teenage Worrier's LIFE. But real lasting Depression, like when you know you should be pleased that the sun is shining but you can't remember why, because you can't feel pleasure, is serious. No-one should have to put up with feeling like that and it is important to get help. People talk V. Disparagingly about therapy or about 'Happy pills', but both these

things save lives and are essential tools for recovery.
Many many people have tried one or the other to get
them out of a hole and then found that they never
need them again. So don't Worry that if you need
treatment for Depression it is going to be a
LIFElong thing. But do see your doc, fast.

See also PSYCHIATRISTS.

DIETS

EL CHUBB'S DIET TIPS:

1. Eat what you like.
2. Eat when you're hungry.
3. Never read any diet tips except these.

IF everybody had always followed this excellent
advice, sez Dr Chubb, then we wouldn't have tens of
thousands of miserable Teenage Worriers suffering
from Eating Disorders and wishing they looked like
Kate Moss.

BUT

(this is my big 'but', not to be confused with the
dieter's big butt), it obviously ain't quite that
simple.

Why? Because we've all been bullied about food
over the years:

'You can have your pudding after you've finished all your greens' . . . 'Think about the Starving Children in Poor Countries' . . . 'Oooooh! MORE choccy cake! You *naughty* thing' . . .

Then, after a dozen or so years of being made to eat everything on our plates whether we liked it or not, we're told to watch our weight. ARG.

No wonder we're confused.

But if over a third of Teenage Gurlz in Britain (some say as many as 42% – *which is nearly HALF of us!!!!!!!*) are Worried about their weight to the extent of going on DIETS – then we have a *Big* Problem.

Fact is, we need food, we need good food, we need plenty of it. It is making us strong, healthy and clever.

You need loads of vitamins, protein and minerals and you can get them by eating loads of healthy food.

COUNTING CALORIES:

A calorie is a unit of heat. Which means energy. Some food has more, some less. Counting calories does not help you find out whether the food has other good stuff in it, like minerals and vitamins. It is also so V. Boring. Can you imagine counting leaves on a hedge? But magazines are badgering our mothers to do this on every news stand. And Teenage magz and TV programmes do the same by

Eat some of these each day to be ~ HEALTHY ~

Some DAIRY-ish bits.
(cheese, yoghurt, milk)
~~TWICE~~ a day.

MEATISH or SEED-ish bits.
(nuts, fishy-stuff, a nice
eggy, chicky or redmeat).
2 or 3 times a day. Could be
peanut butter, f'rinstance.

VEGGIES
Kool cucumber, beans!
Brocolli (v.v. good for you).
Carrots! Etck. 2 or 3 times.

BREAD-ish stuff.
Pasta! Rice! Buns!
Cereal! LOADS.

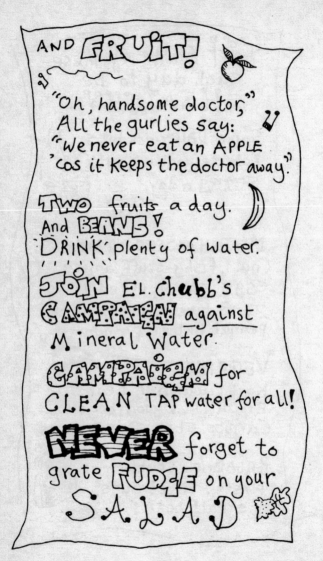

AND **FRUIT!**

"Oh, handsome doctor,"
All the gurlies say:
"We never eat an APPLE
'cos it keeps the doctor away"

TWO fruits a day.
And **BEANS!**
DRINK plenty of water.

JOIN El. Chubb's
CAMPAIGN against
Mineral Water.

CAMPAIGN for
CLEAN TAP water for all!

NEVER forget to
grate **FUDGE** on your
S A L A D

presenting us with pics of UNREAL gurlz.

Campaign for Real Gurlz in all their blobby, stringy, knobbly, floppy, fluffy, gritty, daffy, dottiness! Real Gurlz are Brill!

I'm burbling on about this at some length 'cos I now realize how many gurlz are obsessed with their weight and it is ruining their lives. In fact my own prob is I always wanted to be fatter (so I don't go straight up and down and look like a fireman's pole) but I am beginning to realize that just as we all have different colours, noses, talents, dreamz, Etck, so we are all different weights and your natural body weight is what you will get if you just eat and exercise sensibly and enjoy it.

If you are seriously obese and/or very tired, it could be a medical condition like an underactive thyroid, so it is worth asking the doc to check this and anything else out. Don't be fobbed off. Get a blood test (especially if you are also tired). But if you are just plumper than average, who really cares? What is average anyway? (Size 16, so there: that means half the women in Britain are size 16, a quarter are over and a quarter are under.)

Dieting doesn't work. It makes you cold (lack of energy), depressed (lack of fun), it makes you thick (mentally, not physically – it deprives the brain of nutrients). It makes money for ruthless Diet-mongers and advertisers – and it makes for depression in Teenage Worriers.

See also EATING DISORDERS and EXERCISE.

DISABILITIES

Most Teenage Worriers are convinced that they are
riddled with abnormalities of one kind or another –
noses, willies, bazooms Etck too big, not big
enough. This kind of Worrying can feel as though it
is blighting yr LIFE. But the kind of disabilities
that actually render you incapable of doing most of
the things in this buke are the serious ones, so stop
whingeing for once (wish I could) if you have sight,
hearing and a working pair of arms and legs.

Sometimes it might be qu. good for the soul to
pause to ponder on the fortunes of those who don't
have all the werking parts, like Sylvie, the gurl at
my Primary Skule who had Cerebral Palsy and was
sent on to a 'Special Skule' when she was 11 'cos
Sluggs Comprehensive wouldn't take her. Sylvie
could walk a bit (with crutches) and talked using a
machine that sounded a bit like a Dalek. But she
was V.V.V.V. Clever and prob got V. Bored in
her Special Skule. I never kept in touch with her. I
think I'll ring her up now (lash guilt moan).

There *has* been progress recently for better access
Etck and if you have disabilities you can now do
Wheelchair Olympics and suchlike, but the most
important thing is to feel a Proper Person and not
someone who is just identified as blind (or 'visually
impaired' or 'differently abled' or whatever the
fashionable phrase is).

DOGS

If Rover sees me recommending Dogs I'm afraid she'll have a panic attack and leave home. My secret desire to have a Dog is therefore best-kept secret in town so I cannot reveal it even to you, tender Reader. However, many Teenage Worriers unburdened by (I mean, not privileged to own) cats, yearn for a pooch to call their own and some even have mogs that co-exist happily with dogs. I guess there are houses where parents are quite happy about the many exotic mixes of furs and smells that arise from a cosy collaboration between the feline and the canine, but sadly the House of Chubb is not one.

Dogs come in three basic types:

↑ Bunny
rabbit
slippers

LASSIE (dog-of-your-
dreams).

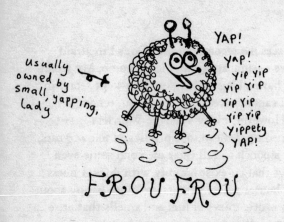

YAP!
YAP!
Yip yip
Yip Yip
Yip Yip
Yip Yip
Yippety
YAP!

Usually owned by small lady

Yapping,

FROU FROU

FANG

DRAMA

All Teenage Worriers act and most, let's be heartbreakingly honest, are Drama Queens. Gurlz and Boyz pose before mirrors for hours in vain attempt to simulate Sean Beanpole, Brad Pittbull, Meryl Sleep Etck, usually by adopting Visage like person torn between conflicting sensations of Erotic Trance and Seasickness, in hope of getting on fast track to flame and gory.

El Chubb hates to disillusion any Stagestruck Worrier with boring, Adult-type statistics, but, like yr Elders and Worsers are bound to tell you at some point, 92% of actors are out of werk at any one time. That means 8% of actors are marching around shouting famous lines from Spokeshave, being filmed thrashing around in sack with Sharon Grone, Tom Spews Etck, fighting animatronic dinosaurs, blowing things up Etck, and the rest are languishing on dole.

Since even the 8% who are werking all the time are V.V. Insecure and spend all their time Worrying if enough people have noticed them, this means they never stop and they go on taking werk that the other 92% wld really like – frinstance a nice little voice-over on an advertisement for mashed potato that anyone cld do, but it always goes to a Famous Voice. The message is: 'Eat mashed potato and get as big a house/car/willy/bank balance/fan club as Sean Beanpole. It worked for him, why not you?'

Forgive me, gentle Reader, for introducing a note of cynicism here. I, too, have my Dreamz, but when you look like a hairpin and sound like a sparrow you have to be realistic, hence I will be werld-famous director instead (ahem), though I may consider becoming a Character Actor in middle age, ie: about 25.

Those of you keen to tread boards, smell greasepaint Etck shld definitely have a go while you are still at skule. Most skules (even Sluggs) have Drama groups and end of year productions and it will give you some idea of whether your germ of talent can be nurtured. Viz: if you are too shy to stand up in front of Ms Drizel the Drama Teacher and spout the Bard, you will not fare well at the National Theatre.

DRUGS

Apart from caffeine (see CAFFEINE) and tannin, most drugs are illegal. Being scared of

a) The Law and
b) The effects

is good enough reason to steer clear in humble opinion of El Chubb. But everyone does it, they say. Not so. Even at Druggs – I mean Sluggs – Comprehensive, where they are available to first years like sweeties and men in baseball caps and long mackintoshes hang around outside the playground or send in innocent kids to sell them, even THERE in the cesspit of Urban Dekay Etck *most* of my frenz aren't taking anything. Lots of others are, of course. But increasingly you get respeck for saying 'No' as the Drug Culchur is getting less Kool as more people see their elder cousins, siblings Etck cracking up (literally) from having over-indulged.

Not so much is known about newer drugs, but psychotic behaviour, hallucinations, possible brain damage, depression and kidney damage are real possibilities. As is a terminal visit from the Grim Reaper.

My Aged Father is deeply hypocritical about this – 'Don't do as I do, do as I say' Etck. But I think too much dope in his student days is prob the reason he is now reduced to staring vacantly at *CITYSCAPE* for aeons. Must check this with doc. Also V. Worried whether I had too much Calpol, antibiotics Etck as Baby and am now prey to Killer Viruses Etck. Worry, Worry.

LEGAL DRUGS:
Favoured abuse-systems of adult werld

BOOZ

(though fags giving way to gum).

103

CHAPTER FIVE
EEEEEEzze and FFFFFFze

Have left house excruciatingly early for four whole days in order to avoid dread bus stop and possible nightmarish vision of Adam Stone entwined with Candice Carthage. Know it's crazy when have only spoken two words to him, but confidence at low ebb Etck.

However, this a.m. was V. Late – as usual no kind parent offering lift because

a) Apology for car not working (apology for Father has removed gearbox and left it with No Problem Mate garage, who now don't return his phonecalls about it)

b) Even if it was working Only Father wld deliver lecture about how he walked 6 miles to skule and all he ate was a piece of toast and dripping which had to last him a week.

To cut a short story long, decide to take courage in both flippers and get usual bus. Probably wouldn't see Adam anyway, who cares if I do, just another bloke Etck Etck. Leap full tilt onto bus, hooking strap of bag round bus conductor's upraised warning arm, hurl Self into last remaining seat, dragging bus conductor unwillingly into V. Embarrassing Head In Lap pose. In said circs, look up to Encounter twin orbs Etck of Adam Stone.

'Hi,' he says, as conductor regains dignity with expression clearly registering regret that Page Three-style Bimbette further up bus hadn't provided similar opportunity. 'I haven't met your friend.'

'Eff, orf, sunshine,' proclaims bus conductor artistically, disappearing upstairs in huff.

I am speechless.

'Remember me? We met on the film course.'

How could I forget? Is he really this modest? Etck.

'Every time I see you you make me glad I don't have a baby brother.'

'Even this time?' I stutter.

'Well, I imagine that's his breakfast down your front.'

I always spill my cornflakes but I wasn't about to admit that to A. S. Instead, we fell to relaxed (YES!) chatter.

Chatter chatter we went as if we had known each other for years. I decided I would miss my stop and go wherever he was going but he ruthlessly leapt up two stops before I was due to get off. This was the parting of the ways, then.

'You must come to the next lesson. Candice's father's going to give us a talk. I know he makes appalling films, but how can you resist?'

And, in a blur of blackberry curls and whirling limbs, Adam Stone was gone . . .

All day at skule I am taking advice, mostly from Aggy, but some from lesser mortals. I even consider asking Spiggy and am amazed and slightly shaken to find she is returning to Australia till half-term at least and maybe for ever! Something to do with a sick grandfather. She is

V. Upset and I experience a microsecond of sympathy for her before recalling her betrayal of moi *with Daniel. I don't ask how he's taking her departure but she tells me anyway: how he swears Undying Lurve till end of time and will be writing daily, visiting soon Etck Etck, bore bore. My heart is as stone. Stone. Stooooooone. Adaaaaaam Stoooooone. Swooooooooon.*

Here is my train of thought, roughly:

a) **Glad to say** *Adam recognized me*

b) **Sad to say** *he saw me as pathetic victim of domestic strife, accident-prone luny, or (worse!) pitiful sekshul predator of bus conductors Etck*

a) **Glad to say** *he asked me to go to lesson*

b) **Sad to say** *reason for (a) was only to hear Candice's father speak. Note familiar use of 'Candice', who he obviously knows like back of gland Etck.*

a) **Glad to say** *that he thought Carthage senior made terrible movies*

b) **Sad to say** *(a) prob means that he sees Candice as subtle & delicate flower that needs wresting from vicious & brutish Hollywood climate and rearing in tender fields of Art, Poetry Etck.*

However, must admit to being somewhat intrigued at idea of hearing Mogul Mogul Junior Third actually speaking in the flesh, not to menshun discovering whose flesh he's speaking into, arf arf. Maybe he cld get me Brad Pittbull's autograph? Also wld be a big star with Benjy's frendz Etck and they wld crowd round asking me secret of how the Rocket *in* Stradivarius IX *turned into a pirate ship Etck.*

Temptation beckons, urge to sup with Devil Etck. Might learn how to make mega-bucks or maybe other thing that rhymes with same, wld be definitely more interesting than Sleeve, shld forget Lurve to pursue career anyway and isn't werk a search for Lurve in another form after all? Etck Etck.

Decide to sleep on Big Decision, but BD out with someone else. Anyway, do not get much sleep as it happens, as return home to find message on newly installed ansaphone for my Only Mother from NEVILLE! Arg. The student she spurned for Father! Should I wipe the tape? Have just decided it is best course of action to save Only Mother from Self when she sweeps in and plays message with faint Mona Lisa type smile hovering at extremities of lips. Something about seeing her next weekend! Arg!

'*Who's Neville?' innocently asks El Chubb, super-sleuth, newshound Etck.*

'*Just a friend' is her enigmatic and nerve-wrenching reply. I don't care how many second homes our Neville has got. I DO NOT want a step-father. Only Father suddenly seems the dearest person in werld. I make him cup of tea with a tea bag so strong the only reason you cannot stand the spoon up in it is because the spoon is decomposing too fast, just how he likes it, and tiptoe upstairs thinking how sad it is for him to have married a woman who likes china tea with lemon and is about to leave him for a poncey komputer salesman. I trip over Rover on stairs so Father only gets half a cup, but he is touchingly grateful none the less. To think he invested a fortune in the ansaphone so he could get messages about interviews Etck re his buke and the only call is from my Mother's fancy man! Should I tell him? But no, better to wait and see . . .*

To add to my domestick Worries, Benjy claims there is a patch of carpet just by his bed that he doesn't like the look of AT ALL. He is convinced that after midnight it becomes a quicksand ready to swallow him up. Only Father claims he has taken up enough floor coverings to try to soothe Benjy's phobias and enough is enough. So marshmallow-hearted El Chubb to rescue yet again . . . I promise to come into Benjy's room after midnight and wake him up and stand on the patch to prove it is not a quicksand and he becomes completely hysterical.

'No Letto. Nonono Letttooooo. It will wallow you all UP!!!'

Are all families as mad as mine?

EARTH

This is all we got so we better look after it.
    See ENVIRONMENT.

EASTER

Easter is ye time for unbridled Chocolate Worship

This card looks V. Rude...

Egg-
shaped
hole.

... until you open it!

Happy Easter

which is V. Good news for most Teenage Worriers
and OK for *moi* although I wld rather the eggs were
made of fudge. The reason we celebrate Easter
Sunday is that for Christians it is the day that Jesus
rose From The Dead. This is a V. Cheery thought
for those of us who hope for a LIFE After Banana,
but does not explain how Easter Bunnies, egg-
rolling Etck came into the picture. I used to think
egg-rolling was about rolling the stone back from
Jesus's tomb, but in fact it dates from Pagan times
as it was part of the original celebration of Spring

Nonsense dear, there's no such thing as the Easter Bunny

(ie: Spring equals new LIFE, so does an egg, so does Jesus's resurrection, so it all fits V. Neatly).

However, even the new Improved totally anti-diet El Chubb does panic at Easter. For the sight of Benjy and his chums overdosing on sticky heaps of eggies, bunnies, chocolate motorbikes Etck is not a pretty sight.

Last year we were up all night as after the Egg-hunt Benjy declared there were still several eggs hiding in his bed. Then he wept copiously because he had bitten the head off a chocolate teddy and thought the Teddy Police wld come for him and throw him into a dungeon with a hot chocolate floor. He fell into a fitful sleep complaining that his chocolate lawyer was demanding his pocket money for the next 500 years . . .

EATING DISORDERS

The main ones are Anorexia, where the sufferer starves, or Bulimia, where the sufferer binges and then throws up. (I have seen my Adored Father exhibit the latter symptoms, but I don't think he has Bulimia Nervosa, more like Alcoholia Ferocia.) They are common among young gymnasts and dancers, and Gurlz seem to suffer more than Boyz, but all kinds of people can get them. These illnesses can start quite gradually, with you just thinking you want to be thinner, or feeling V. Fussy about yr food. You can then get obsessed with the idea you are fat (wafer-thin anorexics feel like this!) and/or greedy. If you are bulimic you may sometimes eat huge amounts (sometimes as much as 30 times what you would normally eat) and then feel disgusted with yourself and make yourself sick. There are many complex reasons for this kind of misery and they are not ones you can disentangle on yr own. So if you think you are suffering from either of these disorders or you have a frend who is, it is V.V. Important to get help.

See also DIETS.

ECLIPSE

Rare occasion when moon blots out sun. This is how you feel when yr True Lurve leaves you for another. Your sun has gone out and All Hope is eclipsed. If, however, you are lucky enough to have a beLurved on 11 Aug 1999, you may wish to watch the next total eclipse that will be visible from Britain. I have already written it in my 5-year diary, so that I can watch it with Adam Stone. You will only be able to see it from Land's End, according to astronomers, or possibly even further out, but I'm sure Adam walks on water, and anyway it's even more Romantick down in ancient mysterious Cornwall, full of Hobbits, Hibbits, Bloggits Etck. I will be *filming* it, whether there is a man by my side or not.

EGG

What is an egg doing in an A–Z of LIFE? Will Men in White Coats remove El Chubb before end of buke? No, I put this in to remind you that this is where we come from and that Female Teenage Worriers produce an egg every month once they've started their periods. And that these little eggs, if they meet a squirmy sperm, can develop into miniature Worriers in a flash, though it akshully takes more than a flash to bring this state of affairs about, arf arf. So be warned! Keep Yr Eggs to Yrself until you feel you're good and ready, feel reasonably sure this event isn't going to undermine Yr Hopes & Dreams, and pref V. Rich with large garden, servants, soundproof rooms for little *enfants* Etck.

See SEX.

ENGINEERING

This has usually been thought of as something only Boyz do, but recently things have started to change. Some Gurlz are becoming car designers, astronauts Etck, and have become V. Cross at the idea that widgets, sprockets Etck are things that only Boyz are interested in. This does of course lead to the possibility that Gurlz cld go on about these subjects in just the same head-banging manner that some Boyz do, which I'm not sure wld be a Good Thing.

Engineering is V. Imp in a technological society like ours, because if Good Engineers don't make things that are better for as many of us as possible, Bad Engineers will make it a lot worse. However, be warned. If you become an Engineer, you may have to get yr Worrying under control. It's not much good calculating the structure of the tallest building on the planet if you're going to lie awake every night waiting for the news that it's fallen down.

Campaign for more Gurl Engineers, Electricians Etck. We can understand this stuff just as well as Boyz. (NB Thought of El Chubb: funny how feminism tends to campaign for more Gurl

THE TEENAGE WORRIER'S GUIDE TO LIFE

politicians, doctors, lawyers Etck but neglects
electricians, road sweepers Etck.)

ENVIRONMENT

Our planet is all we've got. So Teenage Worriers
had better Save It from Ozone destruction,
Deforestation, Vast piles of plastic, Nuclear
dumping, Extinction of species Etck Etck.

When I heard that plastic couldn't be recycled I
panicked, I must admit. Look round yr room at this
very moment and see how much is made of plastic.

In El Chubb's room:

Light fitting
Batman figures (why are Benjy's Batman figures
always in my bed?)
Pens (26, only 2 working)
Pen tops (22, none of which match pens, above)
Walt Disney Ice Spectacular Mug (also eco-hazard
since covered with unsavoury coat of green fur)
Fizzo bottle
Bubblo bottle
Puke-o bottle
Assorted tubs and tubes of glup
Horrible holiday sandals (the holiday was horrible
but the sandals are much worse)
Revolting hair slides
Combs (6)

Brushes (12 . . . guilt . . . why can I never find
one when I want it?)
Toy horses (for any Boyz reading – I got these
when I was 7)
Mini chest of drawers (must look inside – urg –
maybe not)

Strange roundish thing with wobbly bit
Cheapskate *Little Princess* bedhead (I thought this
was pukey even when I was 10 but attempts to
paint it ended in curious marbled effect which I
rather like now).

And so on and on. Benjy's room is much worse and
the kitchen is a disaster area. If this amount of toxic
waste exists in our humble home what hope is there
for entire planet?

EL CHUBB'S ENVIRONMENTAL TIPS:

* Look at aerosol cans to be sure they don't contain
CFCs, which contribute to greenhouse effect,
warming of earth so ice caps melt, ice cream
melts even before you can eat it Etck.

* Dispose of rubbish in bins or take it home. My
Adored Father verges on Road Rage when driving
behind people who throw wrappers out of their
car windows, though shld the conflict come to
court, it wld be as well the opposition lawyers
shldn't see the room he works in.

* Join an environmental protection group like
Greenpeace or Frenz of the Earth. Even the
pittance you can spare them helps to challenge
Big Bizness, Dodgy Govts Etck on damage to the
planet that might make our lives as future Adults
and parents V. Unhappy.

* Do not pick yr nose and wipe it under the desk.
This is V. Damaging to skule eco-system, and

possibly to Yr Own Personal Ego-System if
discovered by Adored One who has previously put
you on a pedestal Above All Others, some hopes,
gripe, moan, whinge.

EUROPE

Geography has always been my V. Worst subject
because I have geographical dyslexia, a rare medical
condition invented, perfected, researched and
suffered nobly by El Chubb. I know London is near
the bottom of the British Isles and that Scotland is
at the top and that Wales is on the left and that the
whole lot looks like an old man with a beard. That's
about it, but as we shamble towards European
Union, linked to ye grate Outside Werld by
Channel Tunnel Etck, I realize it is V. Imp to
understand the werkings of the Werld and therefore
to understand how we fit into it. Even more so since
all werk is becoming global now and money leaps
about the place electronically and Wicked
Financiers put it where people are prepared to slave
for 25 hours a day for one kopek Etck.

European dyslexia is a much more widespread
disease than Geog Dys (see above) and is suffered by
most of our politicians and nearly all citizens over
30. They want to be on a nice little tight little
island and certainly don't want bossy foreigners
telling us that we should be giving blokes paternity

leave, or paying better pensions or other wimpy things like that. I have V. Sneaky feeling that Europhobia is about not wanting other folks to see how stingy, poor Etck we are. On *le autre main*, as they say in France, we need to preserve National Culchur Etck as well as next nation. Yeeeeech. Olé! Mon Dieu! Écu! Etck. I am going to werk V. Hard to learn more about how it all werks.

EXAMS

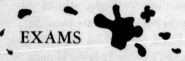

Grue, yeech, screech, gnash Etck. Exams are coming back in a big way in Our Soc, and Adored Mother is V. Upset about the pressure it will put on poor ickle Benjy having to sit SATs (if you follow me) at the tender age of 7 Etck, when all she had to do in skule at that age was occasionally splash a bit of paint over herself or act out a day in the life of an aardvark Etck, but then only if she really wanted to. I have realized from the only meagre few posh frendz I have (ie: Hazel, Hazel's brother and, once – sob – Daniel Hope) that getting into Oxford, Cambridge Etck is not simply a matter of yr native wit and brilliance (otherwise me, myself, *moi* would be there already of course, some hopes) but how determined yr teachers are to train you to do exactly what examiners want instead of Express Yrself. I have even heard of expensive cramming skules where the lessons are all different according to which entrance exam yr

parents are putting you through, instead of
Unfolding Vistas of Wondrous Knowledge about
Werld Etck. Is this what Edukashun is for? I ask
*moi*self.

But, however little they may reveal about YOU,
the One True Person, exams are the way the system
sorts out the people there might just be enough
decent jobs for (and even this seems to be a fading
hope) and you need to put some time and effort into
them if you are not to end up in cardboard box,
being dragged around by dog on piece of string
Etck. Just dream of Riches Untold, Werld at Feet,
washing in asses' milk Etck. By no means all of the
people now living this lifestyle have been much
good at exams, viz Royal Family, pop stars,
footballers Etck, but since jobs of this kind are very
few and far between, you need to narrow the odds on
the ones that are left, ie: forget LIFE's joys for one
year for GCSEs and two years for 'A' levels.

See also SCHOOL.

N.B. Walk to school unless moving
pavement, designed by El Chubb,
(patent pending) is available
near you.

EXERCISE

If you're walking to skule and back, doing some
sport and swimming (about half an hour three times
a week in all) you should be getting enough exercise
and you are unlikely to be fat. Largely due to the
influence of slobs like *moi* who think it's kool to get
out of swimming Etck by mimicking agonizing

119

Right. Up, down.
Up, down. Up. Down.
S-T-RETCH. Phew.
Think I'll leave the
other eyelid till tomorrow

period pains 'cos actually we are just too embarrassed to reveal our concave bazooms Etck in the changing room, Sport for Gurlz has had a low profile in the lives of Teenage Worriers.

Who WANTS to do a zillion sit-ups in three seconds; gallop through freezing mud and scratchy brambles (OK if you're on a horse); get kicked in shins chasing after ball with mind of its own or knocked unconscious by oaf with hockey stick? Us Kool Gurlz can think of better things to do, like varnishing our fingernails, peeling a grape and giggling in corners . . .

WELL . . .

that's what I used to think.

After my own dazzling skills at football went unremarked by teachers who discouraged Gurlz' teams (I'm glad to say this is one thing that's *beginning* to change . . .) I went into a sulk and found lifting the TV channel changer was about my exercise limit. But then along comes a lot of V. Convincing Evidence that exercise is good for you in lots of ways: not only does it keep you bouncy physically – and therefore less likely to suffer an early banana – but it also helps you concentrate, relax, feel happy and improves confidence. Well well.

Obviously the above is not true of crazed Middle-aged Worriers who kit themselves out in fluorescent lycra to burn off calories on horrible-looking machines or let themselves be bullied by poisonal [*should that be 'personal'? – Ed*] trainers.

El Chubb's version is: Lurve yr body enuf to take it for a brisk walk, refreshing dip in heated pool, frisky gambol with cat, dog Etck three or four times a week. Have supply of fudge handy to keep energy supplies up.

Campaign for equal sports facilities for gurlz and boyz and don't be a wimp if you fall over, or lose. Games are supposed to be fun.

TYPICAL TEENAGE WORRIER'S EXERCISE REGIME:

7.10 a.m. Turn off alarm, pull pillow V. Sharply over head (exercises arms).

7.45 Shout back at parent that you have been up for hours. Shamble guiltily out of bed (whole bod, including lungs).

8.00–8.20 Usual masticating (this means *chewing*, you rude thing), scrubbing, flapping about stuff that gets some clothes on and food in bod.
Rest of day: skuley stuff. Pretend to have agonizing period cramps and so avoid any compulsory sport.
Evening: Bits of masticating, shambling, flapping, as for morning. Some channel changing.

   NB Aerobics is where you keep moving enough to raise heart beat Etck for 20 minutes and is popular refuge of Middle-aged Worriers. OK if large quantity of fudge consumed between bouts.
   See also SPORT, WALKING.

EYESIGHT

Aggy first realized she needed glasses when she got on a bus to skule and ended up on a sightseeing tour of the Changing of the Guard. She still didn't go for an eye test, though, until about three of her frendz had decided she was a stuck-up old bat because she never said 'hello' to them in the street. The final straw came when she failed to recognize one of her aunties, who immediately started a Bad Behaviour and Yoof of Today speech which sent her chasing off to the Optician.
   If you can't see bus numbers you are probably short-sighted. If you can't read small print you are probably long-sighted. Either way, it's best to get it

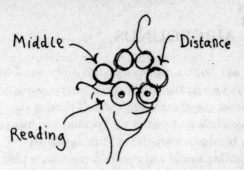

Make a spectacle of yourself with L. Chubb's REVOLVING SPECS-for-all-Reasons

checked as you will be more of a social outcast if you ignore your frenz, catch wrong buses, or can't read the paper than you wld be in glasses. And you can always save up for contact lenses later if you really feel bad about having specs, although about one in five teenagers need them, so it's not that unusual. And in the humble opinion of El Chubb, they look V. Interllekshual and Kool, especially new designer frames Etck which some kids are now wearing with plain glass in them. Weird.

I always fancied Clark Kent more than Superman, myself, and Aggy's goggles, which really are V.V. Thick pebble-type glasses that remind you of little cottage windows or those dimpled beer mugs, certainly never put Daniel Hope off. Sigh . . . gnash. Maybe I shld get a fake pair to convince Adam Stone that although I may not have the allure of Ms Navel, I am instead a dashing interllekshual . . .

Fairgrounds

Still El Chubb's big tip for a fun night out. I have always Lurved the tinkle of the Merry-go-round, the squeal of the ghost train, the dull thud of the wooden ball as it misses the coconut and hits yr ickle brother – even the sad little goldfish swimming round and round in their little plastic bags . . . Why is it, when I hate getting ripped off by manky advertisers, diet-mongers, cosmetics con-artists, I don't object to getting ripped off by Fairgrounds?

After all, you KNOW, when you try to get the ring over the pink panda, that it will never fit over the big wooden box that the panda is sitting on. You KNOW, when you fish with your little wooden stick for the plastic duck that it will NEVER be the duck that wins the LIFE-size toy gorilla . . .

But the great thing about the Fairground rip-off is that people who run fairgrounds are really *working* for it. They're driving around in caravans, unpacking enormous generators, putting up stalls, wiring up dodgems, cranking big wheel handles and shouting their heads off to convince you it's worth spending a quid on a ride.

Also, at any decent Fairground, you get something if you lose. Who cares if the fluffy toy is worth a quarter of what you paid to throw the darts? Benjy will still be thrilled with its little green face and furry claws.

FASHION

For the last year, what I facetiously refer to as my 'wardrobe' (ie, that is: three sweatshirts, three joggers, three T-Shirts) has always been in the following shades: sable, ebony, jet and fog. I am considering branching out into subtle shades of mist and cloud for Spring.

Jumpers are what some
Teenage Worriers wear
when their Mothers feel cold

However, I always add my own personal touch, ie: waistcoat, jumper with hearts on, and make exception for pair of jeans. The outlay for this wardrobe, which suits all occasions, was £24.50 since everything but the jumper (knitted by Granny Chubb) came from charity shops.

Now hearken to me, any of you Kooltypes who think this sounds sad. Even ye grate Supermodels dress this way. They are so bored of the posh designer label type stuff they have to ponce about in all day for photographers that they like to relax in nice homey stuff that is Theirs Alone (even if it was someone else's before). More Imp, designer stuff goes out of Fashion V. Kwick, so if you want to

Chuse Yr own
Luke

avoid going out of Fashion take El Chubb's advice and never be IN Fashion in the first place.

Create yr Very Own Look. For some, it may be polka dot headscarves and frilly petticoats. For others, a beige tube, unadorned. Some may even like a little jumper for the face so that they can look out at the werld without the werld always looking in. Little hats for ears may become a common fancy. Or large green galoshes, resembling a frog. Why not?

El Chubb sez there is a conspiracy of sameness that tries to force penniless Teenage Worriers to empty their pockets into the maw of the Fashion Industry. Join El Chubb's Campaign against Designer Labels! Or invent yr own.

See JEANS, TRAINERS.

FEDORA

V. Nice hat as worn by Humphrey Bogart in *Casablanca* (one of the movies on your 'must-see' list). Which wld suit Adam, I think.

FEELINGS

Feelings are supposed to be a V. Imp part of being a Yuman Person, but when you're a Teenage Worrier you can do with a few less of them, because they seem to keep washing all over you without warning and leave you standing there bedraggled, confused and conspicuous.

But I know my Feelings for my Only Family (speshally my Benjy), for Rover, Adam, my frendz, as well as my Feelings for ye poor, homeless, starving Etck are what go to make up El Chubb, and they're a way of knowing something about the World that I ought to trust as much as any other way of knowing or explaining things. If we lose our Feelings, then we might as well just get ourselves replaced by holograms, put ourselves away in deep-freezes, and save money on Food Etck.

On the other hand, if we are all Feelings and no Judgement, then we can't put ourselves in anyone else's place, which is what babies are like – and Adults who are like that often leave a lot of mess around for other people to clear up, just like babies do. So part of getting your Feelings sorted out is to remember that other people have them too. So protect your Feelings, Teenage Worriers, and they'll look after you!

FIRST AID

All Teenage Worriers shld have access to a V. Good First Aid Kit, ie: one containing slobs, sorry, swabs, loads of different plasters, bandages, antiseptic creams, anti-sting creams, scissors and preferably a

V. Big Medical Dictionary . . .

But nothing beats going on a First Aid course, so I am told, and when I have overcome my V. Laziness I am going to go on one (wish I had had the kind of sensible, pushy parents who made me go to Gurl Guides Etck so I wld have picked up these things when I was young).

The Red Cross and St John's Ambulance run V. Good courses so you can find out what to do if your sibling is choking on a marble and you might actually save a LIFE Etck.

FOOD

See DIETS and VEGETARIANISM.

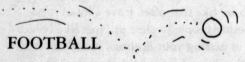

FOOTBALL

A V. Odd thing happens to Boyz aged about 8 or 9. From complete ignorance of sport, overnight they know the names of all the Football players in the werld plus the scores of all the matches that have ever been played. This is proof that the Yuman brain is more powerful than the best komputer, as no-one teaches them this stuff and none of these Boyz has ever been seen to read a buke! HOW does it happen? Boyz then go on to prove that Football is V. Much more interesting than Gurlz for the rest of their LIVES, eg: they will queue for hours in freezing rain to see it, spend all their dosh on related items, be over-moon when it goes their way and cry when it doesn't. When were they ever this moved by Lurve? If you can't beat 'em, join 'em, sez El Chubb. Or at least I did. I was V.V.V. Good at Football at my Primary Skule but they badly discouraged Gurlz from playing and it has left *moi* Scarred for LIFE. Campaign for Gurlz' Teams!! Campaign for Mixed Teams!! I am sure that in a few years' time we will be as good as Boyz at this. All it takes, after all, is Skill

See also SPORT.

FREEDOM

'The condition of being free or unrestricted . . . personal or civic liberty; absence of slave status . . . the power of self-determination; independence of fate or necessity', the dictionary says. Freedom is a V. Complex thing, and it is V. Imp aspect of deciding what kind of World Teenage Worriers want to become Adult Worriers in. Frinstance, when the Cold War ended, bits of Berlin Wall turned into expensive souvenirs Etck, newspapers all said this was a Victory for Freedom, because people in Eastern Europe no longer had to Worry about being watched by secret police, told what job they had to do, denied opportunities to Travel World, wonder what it might be like to have Sky TV, Levi jeans Etck. I must say this does seem V. Boring and Disagreeable way to live yr LIFE.

But now they all have Freedom, and many people in those parts of the Werld can't afford a loaf of bread any more while some are driving round in stretch limos Etck, so some are Freer than others. This is the kind of thing that can make yr Brain Hurt, but I think it's worth hurting it a bit for the sake of becoming Better Citizen.

I have a personal rule about Freedom, which is not a big new Lightbulb Above Wig thought, but which I try to keep reminding myself about. Treat other Worriers (and even non-Worriers, though LIFE is so much fairer to them they hardly deserve the break) as you wld wish to be treated Yrself. Freedom seems to go Down Plug when people stop thinking of other people as needing the same thingz they do.

♪ FREEEEDOM'S ♪ JUST ANOTHER WORRD for nothing LEFT to LOSE

↑
old folk songs sometimes speak TRUE dept.

FRIDAY

Friday is a V. Confusing day in the anals, sorry
annals, of El Chubb, because it is the last day of the
skule week and therefore a Good Thing, but the
beginning of the weekend, with all its potential for
Worrying Events, non-Events Etck. It takes its
name from Frigg (*with two 'g's – don't be rude*), or
Friia, a character in Norse mythology, the wife of
Odin and mother of somebody called Balder, and
she can't have been much of a mother if she called –
or allowed Odin to call – her son that in the first
place. It's supposed to be a day celebrating marriage,
love and byooty, so it's not surprising I have mixed
feelings about it.

NB Other days of the week info to impress yr
frendz: the days of the Sun, Moon and Saturn
continue in Sunday, Monday and Saturday; the
Anglo-Saxon name for Tyr, the Norse god of war,
survives in Tiw's day (Tuesday); Odin or Woden's
name continues in Wednesday; Thursday originates
from Thor's-day, named in honour of Thor, the god
of thunder.

SO, Worrier's Tips: wear sun-block on Sundays,
Moon about on Mondays, fight on Tuesdays, wear
wode on Wednesdays, wear rubber soles on
Thursdays (in case of being hit by lightning).

FUDGE

Fudge. Fu-u-u-dge. Fuuuuuurge. Say it loud and there's music playing. Say it soft and it's almost like praying. Etck.

If you are a genuine fudge aficionado you must score high in the following TRUE FUDGEFACTs QUIZ:

TRUE FUDGEFACTs QUIZ

1) What is the ideal flavour for fudge?

2) Describe the ultimate FUDGE texture.

3) When should you carry FUDGE?

4) Where should you carry it?

5) What is the best accompaniment to Fudge?

6) If you were a guest on Desert Island Discs, what would your chosen luxury be?

7) If you had to choose between salad dressings, would you choose a) Thousand Island b) French c) Blue cheese d) Grated fudge?

8) Have you ever made your own fudge?

9) How many kinds of fudge have you sampled?

10) Name ten things (not including people or pets) that you prefer to fudge.

FUDGEFACTS ANSWERS

1)FUDGE should be vanilla.

2) It should be soft with only a hint of crunch on the outer layers.

3)Always

4) Everywhere

5) More fudge

6) A lifetime's supply of fudge.

7) Grated fudge

8)To score a point, your answer should be "yes"

9) To score a point, you should be able to recall at least a dozen different fudges in detail

10) if you can name ten (or even four) things you prefer to fudge, I'm afraid you cannot join L.Chubb's Fudge de Luxe Club.

A score of Ten entitles you to fully paid up membership, plus *Fudge de luxe* badge, certificate, recipe buke Etck. Just make a cheque for £159.99 payable to El Chubb Enterprises Ltd. and await your gorgeous package.

CHAPTER SIX
GEEEEze, HHHHHHHezz and IIIIIIze

Deciding factor about going to film lesson has been to assuage Benjy's misery at losing his Year One skule work, which of course I left behind at the class in my abject confusion and hot desire to escape. My Mother was distraught about it since it contained a Mother's Day card with about 8 zillion kisses on it and 'I lov you biger than a cake' V. painstakingly inscribed upside down within. I admit that this is a thing worth keeping but I am V. Frosty with my Mother just now (not that she notices) and am more influenced by the pitiful cries of dear Benjy. Viz:

'S'got my stickers innit. And my picture of a War machine for cutting baddies heads off and then torcherin' the bodies till they confess.' Oh well.

Secretly think I might get chance to show my moving photographs at last, and win Adam's affections away from the dread Candice. But this is a slim hope, since whole class will be agog at the star performance.

5 gurlz I hardly know at skule have given me their autograph bukes to take to Mogul and I am V. Embarrassed but feel it my duty to try, and more importantly they will go round saying I made it all up if I don't . . .

Go home from skule early and try on 5 tops, all of them different shades of black. Decide on darkest, plus fog-

*coloured trousers as on first day, as they are only pair I
have without scorch marks.*

Quake off to lesson.

*Mogul Mogul Junior Third is a vast slab of a man
with voice like motorbike engine, oozing power, wit, charm,
danger Etck and leering at entire class who he obviously
expects to fall into bed with him at flash of gold tooth,
dentist's bills Etck. Makes particular eyes, I feel, at
Adam, as it happens.*

*Tells us all about how he was born in shoe box at
bottom of municipal garbage tip Etck and struggled to feed
his crippled sister on pieces of used takeaway fried chicken
boxes Etck, eking a living by selling fictional maps of
Hollywood stars' favourite nude bathing locations to
tourists from Tennessee. Whilst in intensive care following
one such transaction, Mogul received delirious vision of
man spirited away by space aliens for experiments,
condemned to repeatedly returning to earth as chicken
nugget, vainly attempting to proclaim his difference from
all the rest before asphyxiation by barbecue ketchup and
descent into bowels of gruesome winos Etck. Provides theme
for first great Mogul work,* Close Encounters of the
Slurred Kind. *Know he has made this bit up and that
most of audience hasn't realized, so am beginning to like
him when he skips 20 years and, glancing at his watch,
tells us exactly how much each of his films has grossed at
box office. My writing hand now V. Numb at adding
loads of OOOOOOOOOOOOs to every figure he mentions
and then doubling them.*

Suddenly it's over.

'*Any questions?*' *He can barely conceal his impatience.*
'*Does your sister like your films?*' *I bravely jibber.*
'*Never asked her.*' *He laughs a scornful laugh exactly
like a villain in a horror movie, as if to teach us that
scraping yourself up to top of ladder from V. Humble
beginning does not necessarily make you a Nice Person. He
sweeps out with Candice under his giant, batlike wing.
Everyone else sweeps after him, waving autograph books.
Sleeve is quivering with fulfilment. No sign of Adam.*

All is lost.

A hand on my arm. '*Let's get out of here.*'

*I turn to gaze into twin orbs, coal dark with twinkling
fires in depths. Etck.*

'*He was even worse than I thought,*' *laughs Adam,
dazzlingly. Swooooon.*

Adam Stone and I GO FOR A COFFEE.

*We talk for two hours about Art, Poetry, the Mysteries
of the Yuniverse, Etck. Adam cares nought for power or
money, but only how to forge a Better World Etck. He
Lurves my photographs!*

Most amazing of all, he has asked me to go to Large
Door *with him tomorrow night!!!! It is apparently a V.
Grate black and white movie of the kind Adam and I
(how easily that little couplet tinkles on my tongue) Lurve.
I have found a soul mate! As we part, he gently squeezes
my hand, a light brush of flame, a millisecond of Perfect
Bliss.*

*Luckily, tomorrow is Friday and I am allowed to go
out with Aggy. I can easily put her off and sneak to*

cinema without embarrassing questions from nosy parents.
My cup runneth over. I float on wings of pashione Etck.

GAMBLING

A V. Bad thing, say the Fingerwaggers in
Authority. The way to a life in a cardboard box, or
even a wooden box.

And we are all encouraged to do it. From that
first crisp packet that says 'Win £200 if you can find
a blue crisp inside', all the way up to the National
Lottery which makes people believe they have a
chance of winning gazillions, and lets Govt off hook
re funding stuff it thinks is trivial, like The Yartz.

I wouldn't mind all this hypocrisy from the Adult
Werld if

a) People weren't spending more than they can
really afford of their Income Support on the Lottery
and

b) Winning 8 million quid made people feel
happier, which to judge by newspaper stories of
families falling out, winners going mad Etck it
doesn't always seem to.

See MONEY.

All moi
needs is
an Ace of
Hearts
(sigh)

GARDENS

Gardening is the favourite pursuit of Middle-aged Worriers. If they can't stumble around with an old trowel in a silly-looking hat, then they will listen to V. Old people with lurching country accents burbling about it on the radio. But getting your mitts stuck in the earth is V. Good for soul whatever your age, and for sheer entertainment I dare you to listen to a Gardening programme on the radio. (Yes! Radical!) Far from being quiet, purring programmes, everyone always disagrees with each other: a little old lady from Godalming will ask what the best treatment for her wilting *Rosaria lavabo* is and . . .

Dr Pete Bogg will insist she needs more acid in her soil and a sprinkling of rotten cow bones every second Tuesday. He will be contradicted by Crumbilia Barke, with a sturdy assertion that *Rosaria lavabo* must never be treated with anything on Tuesdays and that it needs considerably less, rather than more acid. In wades Farmer Slurry, robustly denying everything that has gone before and saying that his favourite plant is the *Rosaria lavabo*, a Thing of Byooty and a Joy For Ever: he had one growing outside his only windowsill when he was a young boy without shoes or toys in the West Country and what he loved most was the smell of the *Rosaria lavabo* as it wafted up through the cow dung of a Summer's Morn . . . We move on to

Professor Thorn, who briskly says he loathes the *Rosaria lavabo*, doesn't think it's worth growing, especially not in Godalming where the soil is too earthy. Also, he feels that cow bones are spreading BSE causing Mad Plant Disease, in which cucumbers think they're personal vibrators and turn pink. He would grow a nice cactus instead and can recommend several varieties. Instead of leaving in a huff, the sweet little old lady from Godalming thanks them kindly and goes home to her beloved *Rosaria lavabo* none the wiser, but replete with the satisfaction of having her question addressed by the experts.

There are two important LIFE-Skills here for the Teenage Worrier:

1) You don't have to know the answers, you just have to SOUND as if you do.

2) Regional accents are an advantage in Gardening Experts.

However, LIFE can be enhanced by Gardens: planting runner beans, frinstance, is V. Rewarding. You get seeds (qu. cheap) which just look like dried beans and all you do is push them in a bit of earth in the Spring. The result is amazing – like Jack and the Beanstalk they just run right up the little bamboo poles you have also stuck near the seeds and soon they have red flowers and then they have beans! Lots! You only need a teensy patch of earth for this.

GAY

If you prefer same SEX to opposite SEX you are like most fok on planet. BUT, if you like your own SEX

in a sekshual way, you may find you are prone to
Worry, since this is considered by ye grate
unwashed public as not NORMAL. Since V. Little
that I do (ie: praying in public highways, bending
down to touch floor at odd moments, turning lights
on and off twice) is also considered not normal I
have much empathy. But in my view being Gay is
just like being anything else. It's part of who you are
and the werld is slowly but happily coming to
realize this. If you are lonesome though, you need
mates who are also Gay. If you can't find any easily,
join a group, ring a helpline Etck.

GERBIL

Horace's
cousin.

Sweet-looking, inoffensive (except in case of Horace)
pet who will do if you can't afford horse or dog. Like
hamsters they enjoy running round on wheels and
shredding stuff.

GONDOLA

No Dream of LIFE is complete without a trip on a
gondola up the canals of Venice singing one
cornetto. Venice will prob have sunk without trace
by the time I have enough dosh to afford this. I
wonder if Adam's folks are rich? (Although of course
I wld Lurve him anyway, Etck.)

GRAMMAR

grammar is a boring waste of time people say its v imp to learn speling punctuation past participles adjectives nouns adverbs sentences paragraphs and all those tedious things because if you dont you wont be able to a get a job b keep a job c make yourself understood d feel like the intelligent worthwhile person you are e get LIFE skills to enable you to make sense of what youre reading now or anything else and also although its often v boring at the time it does make you think that all the people who invented this rich and wonderful language of ours which is all of us over several centuries by the way are v clever and it would be a pity to let it all go down the plug because we cant be bothered to learn a few rules about full stops sometimes i would like it if my teachers didnt scribble all over my werk correcting it all the time so that i could just go with the flow i am now wondering whether the time has come to end this ramble since it is v tiring not putting in any punctuation i am surprised to find its easier to do it the right way i think i have learned an important LIFE skill and instead of moaning i will try v hard to be a better person etck etck moan whinge by the time i have finished this buke i will be a boring old f— who thinks everyone should dot their is and all that old rubbidge.

GUILT *, worry, worry, guilt, worry ....*

Teenage Worriers are prone to Guilt because as well as Worrying about all the terrible thingz that might happen to *us*, we Worry about all the terrible thingz that might happen to everyone else, which we believe we've caused by being too lazy/selfish/ignorant/demanding/indifferent to Fate of Werld Etck. Viz: 'If I had given 50p to Frendz of the Earth instead of spending it on fudge another whale wld be alive today' . . . 'If I had given Benjy a second piece of fudge he wld not have run out of back door in huff, and thus avoided treading on rake and whacking head' Etck.

LIFE-Advice about Guilt is that LIFE isn't perfect and therefore people won't be Happy, free from disasters, bad news Etck all the time, so there's no point in feeling Guilty about yr failures to prevent something that might have happened anyway.

Guilt does exist for a reason, though, because it is part of our CONSCIENCE and a Conscience is a vital part of being a Yuman Bean, stopping us doing bad thingz, or helping us put them right.

HABITS *twitch... tic.... gulp*

Habits and Worriers often go hand in hand, and sometimes they couldn't be prised apart with a crowbar. Habits are, of course, thingz that you do repeatedly, and you may be aware of them or not. Some Habits are OK, because they look Kool. Other Habits are not Kool, like praying all the time in public and hoping people don't notice, picking your nose whilst sharing candlelit dinner with Person of Yr Dreamz, eating chips out of newspapers while snogging Etck. (Though V. Trashy Habits *can* become Kool with the right people, Garage music, Grunge fashons, Trainspotting-type lifestyle Etck).

Get a Grip on Yr Habits! I wish I cld, but I still

1) Twiddle my fringe
2) Touch things twice
3) Always keep my lucky rabbit's foot in my
   pocket
Etck.

Hanging on to these Habits a bit longer helps to keep me sane, I *think*.

See also PHOBIAS.

HANDWRITING

My handwriting looks like the printouts from an earthquake seismograph being used on a toboggan, and I wish I'd concentrated more on my ps and qs at Primary Skule. It's hard to get better at the ancient age of 15 and I think it's V. Unfair that we all have to write job applications in our own writing as people like *moi* will be thought unintelligent when really we're just lazy (ahem) – I mean suffering, um, co-ordination problems or left/right brain probs. Actually, this IS really mean if you are dyslexic but in my case I just didn't bother. It will be a lot easier for Benjy's generation as everyone will just be e.mailing their life histories and they won't have to use a pen at all.

The quick brown fox jumped over the lazy dog.

Pre-teen-Worrier's handwriting on starting Secondary Skule

Tip. If you write BADLY enough, your SPELLING may not be noticed.

the qinck brown fox jumped over the lazy dog

... and at GCSE lvel

For LIFE-Tricks today, however, I urge you to try and enjoy it by getting an italic pen. This was the most boring present I had last Christmas but, to my surprise, I started enjoying it in Feb when I had the flu and *Sesame Street* was over (I was watching it with Benjy, ahem) and I got it out and started doodling. And it was FUN. I even made a V. Good looking Treasure Map (for Benjy, blush) that looked like it was written by an Ancient Hand. Unfortunately we set light to the furniture shortly after, in attempting to make the map go all brown and parchmenty, but that's another story . . .

HANGING OUT (aka Hanging About In The Street)

Essential LIFE-Skill for Teenage Worriers, deprived of dosh and the chance to make any, is to Hang Around on Street Corners. Whether you decide to Look Threatening or not is down to whether or not you want to:

a) Worry old ladies.
b) Worry Teenage Worriers like *moi*self, who will walk three blocks to avoid a large gang of yelling yoofs who might be qu. harmless.
c) Get moved on by The Bill.

To avoid above means hanging around in smallish groups, with hyena-like smile affixed to yr mug (rather than jackal-type scowl which is common face-in-repose mode). It's a V. Cheap way to have fun. You can:

a) Watch the local talent (no rude remarks per-*lease*).

b) Amaze yrself at variety of yumankind that wanders down average street. Viz: Man with carrier bag on head; V. Tall person of ambiguous gender dragging poodle on string; roller-blading pensioner. And the *clothes*: You couldn't make them up. You think most people have trousers and shirts or dresses on, don't you? Look again.

c) Oh well. How about just, er, talk?

HERMAPHRODITE

What a lot of Teenage Worriers think they might be (ie: neither man nore woman). Gurlz Worry about this if they have hairy chests, deep voices, no periods Etck. Boyz worry if they have high voices, titchy willies, some bazooms Etck. Real Hermaphrodites (the word comes from the union in one body of Hermes and Aphrodite) are V. rare, but it is poss to have hormone imbalances, so if you are worried about any of the above (or other things I have not thought of, like an unconquerable urge to

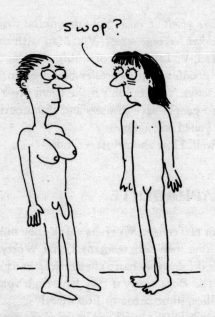

grow a beard, even though you are a gurl) then talk to your doc about it. Hormone imbalances can usually be quite easily redressed and it is worth keeping an eye out, just in case.

BUT it is clearly a Big Prob for your general LIFE-Skills stuff if you don't know which sex you are, or you think you want to be the one you are not. It MIGHT be a good idea if you cld find this sort of stuff out before you had a family . . . or became a vicar or something so you could avoid headlines like FROCK SHOCKS FLOCK. Arg.

HOBBIES

The most imp thingz you can do in LIFE are the things you enjoy. This is one thing many Adult Worriers have forgotten, but it is worth pointing out that men seem better at it than women. Here is an eg of a Sunday morning: Blokes are off to football, or cricket, pottering in sheds, fussing about with fish hooks, sawing up little bits of wood, tinkering with pieces of car Etck Etck. Or maybe watching blokes doing any of these things on TV.

Women are flaffing about with saucepans, irons, dusters Etck, nagging blokes and kids about old socks, fluff Etck. Who is enjoying themselves the most?

I am ashamed to describe this scenario as I am a feminist Etck but it does seem to me that blokes have a better time and not just because they leave all the boring stuff to the women and it's unfair but because they know how to enjoy themselves without feeling guilt (see GUILT).

Even as a young (ahem) teenager, I noticed that there was SOMETHING MISSING from my life that was not missing from BOYZ' lives: *they* were messing about with plastic model kits constructing giant aeroplanes or involving themselves in huge battlefields populated by miniscule warriors with names like Orko the Dread, or, if they weren't out chasing a ball they were at home playing miniature version called SOCKO, HOCKO or CRICKO. It was about this time that we Gurlz started putting away childish things and Worrying. We started to Worry about clothes, Worry about Hair, Worry about Boyz. Arg.

If you have a Hobby, you have El Chubb LIFE-Tricks award-winning potential, which means possible route to happiness.

There are Hobbies and pursuits you do with other people (like Music, Drama Etck – see rest of buke) or there are Hobbies you do on yr own. These are V. Imp for internal serenity Etck and include:

READING
V. Brilliant, as you can have conversations with the author as well as the characters.

Advantages: V. Cheap. In fact, free as long as you get the bukes back to the library on time. Also, you can enter other werlds Etck and this is V. Good for the Soul if the werld you're in is a glume-laden battlefield of divorcing parents, exam-terror, heartbreak or whatever. With a good buke you can

Role-reversal brought on by reading

forget everything – while you're reading.

Disadvantages: people can get V. Snotty about
bukes. I read recently of one mother who said she
would only get her son horror books if he read one
in French (!) for every one he read in English . . . I
wonder if he's still reading anything at all. Middle-
class parents seem to think Enid Blyton or the *Beano*
are somehow bad for kids. V. Weird. If I hadn't cut
my teeth on the *Beano* I don't think I would have
ever got round to Dickens Etck.

Also, teachers and skule can be V. Good but can also help wreck books by looking at them too closely and spoiling the Dream. The Dream is a V. Imp part of the process . . .

DRAWING

Best of all for *moi* as you can literally make anything happen. Most kids draw all the time until they are about 9. Then someone laughs at a picture, or they look at a photograph and see it looks different or some idiot tells them they can't draw and *whoop, zammy!* Away it goes. And with it a lifetime's pleasure.

Drawing should be for fun, not to be a brilliant artist. It really is a hoot making up characters, inventing daft situations, doing squiggles and turning them into objects Etck. Sort of doodling-with-a-bit-more-purpose. There are lots of famous cartoonists who don't draw 'well' in an Art Skule kind of way, but they have a great sense of huymour and somehow that squiggles into the line and – bingo!

Advantages: Cheap – most people can get hold of pencils and paper. Gets expensive if you start graduating to oil paint – but who needs that? This is Hobby time. NB A V. Simple child's watercolour box lasts for ages and you can get loads of good effects.

Disadvantages: Snottiness as above, only along the lines of 'Why don't you do a Still Life, instead of those stupid comic book copies?' To which I reply, 'It may not be Art, but it's still LIFE.'

Adults often think you're wasting time. Being Happy is NOT a waste of time, they're just jealous.

WRITING

Exactly the same as drawing, above. Stories, poems Etck can really help you feel better and also keeping a Diary is V. Good way of venting rage against World Etck.

MAKING STUFF

This can be anything from clothes to sculpture. My own tragick attempts at making trousers last year did nothing for my fashion self-esteem, ditto my attempt at knitting under the patient tutelage of Granny Chubb, than whom there can never have been a better teacher. Even she had to admit that the knotted, multicoloured, fluff-encrusted tube that resulted was more holey than a Gruyère cheese and could not pass as a scarf that even Benjy would agree to plonk under his chin. However, many Teenage Worriers of a more domestic turn of mind like perfect Hazel can run up dazzling little numbers out of bin bags, old sacks, loo rolls Etck and pass themselves off as Supermodels wearing the latest Designer togs without batting an eyelid. And they enjoy it.

The stuff I like making is sculpture from Found Objects. This requires lots of patience but a

minimum of co-ordination as you can stick anything
to anything really. Beach-combing is good for this.
Old starfish are a good find, so are shells and bobbly
seaweed. But what I really like is driftwood that has
been bleached and rubbed by the elements Etck.
You can make great mobiles with this (must see if I
can get a job as a crafts writer on *Adorable Adobis*
magazine – puke). Benjy does a lot of Found Object
stuff: loo rolls, egg boxes, that sort of thing, all
decorated with bits of old wool and milk bottle tops
then left to rot on the kitchen table as my Mother is
too sentimental to ever throw them away . . .

Advantages: V. Cheap. All you have to buy is glue
(not always that easy as newsagents round here
hardly stock any strong stuff 'cos so many Teenage
Worriers are tragickly solving their Lack-of-Hobby-
Situation by getting into a Solvent-Abuse-
Situation).

Disadvantages: You need space. Not available to
moi, sadly. Last week I had to throw out my
beautiful *Serpent Tempting Adam* (ahem), which was
made of a bicycle wheel and 12 old paint tins.

COLLECTING

If you enjoy collecting stuff, it gives you an
identity that makes it V. Easy for people to choose
your presents. Viz: 'Oh, that's old Mary, we can give
her another frog, Dalmatian, egg cup, or whatever.'

Also, a V. Good talking-point for frendz 'Cor!
What a lot of Dalmatians. Where DID you get

Equipment for Making Stuff

1) GLUE (or chewing gum)
2) PAPER (only father's novel)
3) TISSUES, LOO PAPER ETCK.
(pref unused, this is a family buke)
4) OLD EGGS (plus boxes)
5) BITS OF FLUFF
6) GRAVEL
7) BIG BIT OF CARD or WOOD (I used table, but had to cut legs off. Benjy now starving as refuses to eat breakfast off floor, like rest of us)
8 PAINT
9 NICE BITS AND PIECES

INSTRUCTIONS

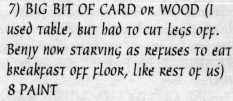

Cover 7 with 1. If using gum, chew well, then dot liberally over surface. Rip up 3 and stick to 7. Add more 1. Chuck handfuls of 5 and 6 at 1. Add 4 and 3. Decorate with 8 and 9.

them all? That one's as big as a hippo. And is this
little chap made of glass? How clever – whoops!
Only one of its kind? Flown all the way from Outer
Mongolia? SO sorry.'

Advantages: Obsessively interesting to the
collector: wherever they are they're on the lookout
and never bored. Means frendz think of you
whenever they see the object you collect. Could be
good for reminding Lurvers of your existence, or
even keeping job in later LIFE. 'We can't chuck
poor Francilla out of her office! Think how much
we'd miss her tea cosy collection.'

Disadvantages: Could be V. Boring for other
people. They are trying to enjoy film, while
Collector-Person wants to rewind video to catch
another glimpse of penguin, priceless jug or
whatever. Expensive. Could be disadvantage for later
LIFE-Skills. 'Either Francilla goes, or her tea-cosy
collection does.'

See also ART, DRAMA, MUSIC, RAINY DAYS.

HOMEWORK

The first, deeply harrowing truth about Homework
is that it has to be done. You cld, as happens in
boarding schools, do yr Homework immediately
after lessons so it's just like a longer skule day, but
most people like to feel skule days don't go on for

ever, so you have to find a way of making yrself do it later, which is V. Hard.

But if you don't, you may feel V. Bad about yrself, if you are truely a Teenage Worrier and not the kind of person who says 'Stuffit' about anything they don't like, and doesn't mind being moaned at all the time.

Why do you feel Bad? Because having your parents/carers/Irresponsible Adults on your back every night is painful and glumey for all concerned.

Fact: Kids in Care often don't do homework. That's because there's often nobody around with the time or involvement in them personally to make them.

Result: These kids do not do so well at skule, and feel rejected all the more even if they act tough and say it's all krap anyway. It's not because they can't; it's just that no-one is helping out.

Good teachers are also V. Good incentives for Homework, because if they make the subject interesting, you want to show them you think it is too. Unfortunately, this is not as common an incentive to do homework as we might like.

There are loads of ways to do Homework, but I've narrowed them down to three basic models – and only one will cure nagging Homework Worry (leading to glume, dume Etck).

MODEL 1
Get home without Hanging Out (see pp. 148). Do

Homework in dazzling firework display of Creative Genius, Brilliant New Ideas Etck. Reward self after with dazzling firework display of Wild Fun, stunning frendz with scintillating wit, Werld Knowledge Etck. Best option if poss but V. Uncommon.

MODEL 2
Get Home. Have snack/watch TV/pick nose. Think about Homework. Go out. Come back (as Homework Worry prevented you enjoying outing). Worry about Homework. Have meal. Watch TV. Worry a lot about Homework. Fall asleep. Wake up V. Miserable.

Do Homework in mop cupboard or on loo first thing in morning, so no-one can see you, but cause general houshold chaos in second case as everyone is banging on door. Resulting work wobbly and somewhat stained.

MODEL 3
Get Home. Have snack. Start Homework. Get diverted by frend, TV programme, enormous emerging pluke bursting through walls of hooter and burying surrounding family in Pompeii-like molten swamp Etck. Follow Model 2 above but for longer and later. Wake up too late and tired to do Homework. But at least you started it, you say to yourself as you wander ashy faced to glumey skule and try to hide from enraged teacher for day.

HORSES

Most noble of beasts, but owning one – and even getting to ride one – is sadly out of reach of yr average Urban Teenage Worrier. Riding lessons are V.V.V.V. Expensive but you can get them by offering to help out at stables or saving a whole year's pocket money for about three lessons Etck. I have been riding four times with Hazel and they have been happiest times of LIFE (sob). Why? I think it's to do with freedom, soul in harmony with beast and nature, wind in hair, all that sort of stuff. And, since Hazel lent me hat, I did not even suffer falling-off terror that you would expect from nachural-born Worrier.

LIFE-long Dream of L. Chubb to own horse currently reduced to proprietorship of four rubber, two plastic, three china and one fake fur model arranged in shambolic cluster on bookshelf above bed. Many hours grooming their ickle manes, making saddles, rugs Etck out of felt and tacky off-cuts of leather have not helped yrs Truely to overcome her Urge. One day, I WILL have that palomino stallion prancing boldly in my meadow . . .

IMAGE

Feeling bad about yr Image? Join El Chubb's Frolicsome Feelgood Group. And take the following Hints and Tips:

Stand in front of a mirror. Describe yourself out loud or write it down, just as though you were describing a sunset, or a building or a bowl of fruit. (OK I know I look like an eclipse, a sky scraper, a squashed banana – help, bananas are now making me think about that word about dying that rhymes with 'breath' – but that's just 'cos I'm in a *negative* mood.) Let's think positive (sweat, grone, massive circulation increase of bludde to single brain-cell Etck). If you don't like something you see, ask yourself why?

So you think you've got a fat nose? Truely? How

**Teenage Worriers before and after positive thinking
NB: proof that poetry is oft based on PAIN...**

fat? Who said so? Are they right? How fat is *their*
nose? What has *your* nose got to do with them
anyway?

Next time you do this, list all the things you like
about yourself. There should be just as many
(how about that 48th hair just above yr left
eyebrow? or that really nice lone eyelash?). Feel
pleased about that eyelash. No-one else will, and it
needs all the Lurve it can get. If it's the only thing
you liked, then ask yrself why?

'Live happily in your body' say the advice bukes. Well, let's not be cynical for a minute (OK, for a second). It *is* poss to feel as though your body is fun – and not just a ramshackle contraption of bits and pieces that have been nailed together anyhow and attached to your soul whether you like it or not.

Good ways of getting 'in touch' (puke) with the 'whole you' (yuk) are exercises that use all your bits, like swimming and yogurt – sorry, yoga – and nice kinds of free zappy dancing (not twiddling around on points and worrying what you look like).

Ever noticed that sporty people are often the most confident? El Chubb thinx (and eggsperts agree) that this is 'cos running about a lot makes lots of little endorphins charge about and these, in their turn, cheer you up. Being fit(ish) means being happy(ish). Getting obsessed with being fit (like all obsessions – sigh) makes you sad. Arg. Must peel self off sofa and exercise ears with gentle flapping before hurling spindly frame into foam bath.

INITIATIVE

You need to show plenty of this to get on in Wicked Cruel Werld. An eg of Lack of Initiative wld be:

Parent: 'What is that strange aroma like boiled plastic?'
Teenage Worrier: 'I think it is the aroma of burnt

plastic, perhaps mixed with a hint of scalded milk.'
Parent: 'Where the F***'s it coming from?'
Teenage Worrier: 'I believe it's emanating from the kitchen.'
Parent: 'What the **** is it?'
Teenage Worrier: 'It seems that the milk saucepan's burnt dry and is now melting.'
Parent: 'Why the **** didn't you turn off the gas?!!!!'
Teenage Worrier: 'Ummmmmmm.'

If you want a teeny chance of getting a job do not be like the Teenage Worrier above (or the parent, either, who should have rushed to stove armed with fire blanket, extinguisher Etck instead of maundering on asking stupid questions and using werds which they would prefer you didn't use yourself). Initiative is obv V. Imp to secure place in labour market Etck.

See JOBS.

INSOMNIA

Trouble sleeping usually means that an average Teenage Worrier is more Worried than usual (or that their ickle brother has had another nightmare re the floor turning into used loo paper Etck). Worry can be caused by over-excitement in Teenagers just as much as in small kids. Even a scary film can do it, or meeting a Lurve-object.

Usual old stuff like warm drinks is best remedy, plus reading V. Old, comforting buke (like *A Pony for Patsy*, which can either make you feel V. Cosy and back on Adored Mother's knee, or so overcome by boredom that you fall asleep in self-defence). Counting sheep always fails for *moi* as I start to get sorry for them all jumping over a gate and then I imagine them jumping over a hedge; then I get interested in how high they can jump and start Worrying whether they will break their legs Etck.

If all these fail and you haven't slept properly for a couple of weeks and have examined your soul for reasons, then it's a good opp to go to doc and pour yr heart out. My doctor always grones audibly at sight of *moi* in waiting room as she is used to me turning up for brain tumours Etck when I have just been wearing too small a hat, or fatal illnesses that most people wld recognize as the common cold. But Insomnia could be due to some quite deep glume and if you are deeply glumey good doctors shld be V. Sympathetic.

INTELLIGENCE

Ours is a Cruel Werld that rates children by IQ tests, crazed exam results, how early they do joined-up writing Etck Etck and neglects Whole Person.

Pause, sez El Chubb, and ask yourself, 'What is

Intelligence?' Is it that which distinguishes (if that's the right werd) us from the animals?

Is it virtue?

Can it be measured?

If so, how can the people with lots of it be encouraged to benefit the rest of us rather than just use it to get rich?

Whether you think you have much of this elusive quality or not, it's clear that it comes in many versions. There's the obvious kind that gets four A* grades at 'A' level and a scholarship to Oxbridge. This kind, however, is often nurtured at the hands of expensive schools and tutors and may lie dormant in the child of a household none of whose members have ever seen the inside of a book.

Then there's the creative kind – that is, good at painting, or music, or inventing. This, too, can be encouraged or crushed by environment. Everyone

Spot the Teenage Worrier with the highest IQ

can learn to play a musical instrument quite competently, frinstance, but most of us never get taught.

Then there's intuitive Intelligence: that's people who are really good at people-thingz, like understanding, consoling, energizing.

Then there's the enquiring kind, full of mad professors and wild physicists. We need these especially for the Teenage Think Tank.

Then there's practical Intelligence – those amazing foks who seem to have been born knowing how to get FM radio on a hairdrier with the addition of a few everyday household utensils.

There is also a growing area of Intelligence to do with survival in The Street – which involves V. Quick assessment of developing situations, ability to change mindsets V. Fast Etck.

I am still trying to discover which, if any, of these Intelligences I possess and so far I have not exhibited the Intelligence to decide. But what I DO know is that developing as many of them as possible is a surer route to Happiness, Fulfilment Etck than developing your body/personality/looks.

Imagine what the articles in *Smirk* COULD look like . . .

Incredible fact: Even if you fed 10 pieces of new information into your brain every *second* you still wouldn't ever fill it up (not even HALF-full) in your whole LIFEtime. The Totally Free Yuman Brain is some awesome komputer.

SMIRK

- *Give Your Intellect a Make-over!* With our ten top tips.
- *Brains are often the First to show signs of Ageing!* Brighten up yours with our IQ Booster-pack!
- *Full Frontal Lobe Workout!* Three easy steps.
- *Dazzle your Man* With Quantum Physics.
- *Curse of the Thick!* How to improve your know-how.

MORE WAYS to FIGHT BRAIN SAG *INSIDE!*

Have feeling this wld make moi feel even more inadequate than beauty tips..

CHAPTER SEVEN
JJJJJJze to LLLLLLLze

Awake on wings of desire Etck in Lurve with whole werld. Werk V. Hard at skule. If only teachers knew how subtle are the yearnings of a Teenage Worrier and that the happier you are, the better you work. Um, not sure this is always true as mooning, moping, day-dreaming Etck are fave habits of Teenage Worriers-in-Lurve. Nevertheless feel V.V.V. Positive.

Get flowers for Granny Chubb on way home, no expense spared Etck. Welcomes bunch of V. Classy roses as 'Lovely daisies', but I am not to be deterred from Positive Mood today, even if she had said they were bunch of miserable weeds she wld not give table-room to Etck.

Make firmer resolution to step up GCSE endeavour and work out ways of earning dosh, though suspect Mogul Mogul did not take GCSEs. Film-directing may not immediately be as lucrative as I had hoped, especially if I follow the dictates of my soul Etck and concentrate on Deep and Meaningful projects involving Angst, long silences, sounds of people making Lurve while camera tracks across Inner City wasteland of dustbins, dead cats (akshully Rover asleep), abandoned sick aunts Etck rather than falling for gloss and glamour of Big Bucks Productions Inc.

Register faintest tremor of disappointment at this

*momentous realization, but impelled to soldier on
nevertheless to new dawn of righteousness (hopefully
marching side by side with Adam Stone, swoooon). Fix up
Hazel's video camera on complicated timing mechanism, so
that it will film Urban Dekay outside my window at
craftily timed intervals during the next few daze for two
minutes at a time. Work out with skill of a thousand
mathematicians that this will allow me SEVERAL
DAZE worth of filming and still leave 10 mins over for
link shots of presenter (moi) talking meaningfully about
passing of time, amassing of dog poo, convening of dossers
Etck. For first time am glad we live in lively area complete
with drug dealers, hookers Etck instead of sleepy suburb
where only street activity comes from soft bounce of kiddies'
pushchairs and only dog poo from refined beumbes of
poodles Etck.*

*Spend happy hour or so designing wooden steps for Benjy
so that he can sleepwalk over quicksand.*

*Feeling of unadulterated bliss somewhat muted by
thought of Only Mother possibly on verge of committing
adultery herself. Is it possible to commit adultery if you are
not married? Get V. Worried and look up adultery in
dictionary:* 'Voluntary sexual intercourse of married
person other than with spouse.'

*Phew. At least my Mother won't be an adulterer, since
she is (tragickly, in my view) not married to my Only
Father. Unless Neville is married. Would that make her
an adulterer? Worry, Worry.*

*Both parents mercifully at home this evening and
apparently talking (or at least grunting) to each other. So*

Rover considering whether Cats can commit adultery
(or whether adults can commit cattery)

*decide to put off Worrying for a day or two and revel in
new-found happiness.*

*Have you noticed, Reader, that I have NOT been
Worrying what to wear for my date with Adam? I am
meeting him in* one hour's time *and I have spent one
hour fixing up video camera and one hour on Benjy's
swamp bridge . . . and this is because, at last, I have
found a boy who I don't have to pretend to be someone else
with. Adam, after all, has seen me covered in purple dye
and cornflakes. He has seen me entwined with a bus
conductor, engulfed by falling cameras, stuffing my fist in
my mouth to stop myself laughing at Mogul Mogul Junior
the Third and blushing violently with the shame of
Benjy's folder. He knows me. This must be the Real
Thing.*

*Er, even so, I'll just spend the next 50 mins ironing my
fog trousers, pressing my Hint-of-Ebony top, running a
quick brush through my eyelashes Etck. And now I run to
meet Him . . .*

Jeans

Denim is V. Sexy on Right Person, but Naff when worn by leering teachers trying to look 'trendy' (a Kool werd from the 1970s that is now only Kool in the same sense as dead frog Etck).

And Jeans, when worn low on cat-size hips of Adam Stone, with tantalizing metal fly buttons Etck (whoops, family buke), remain, as they have done since first cowboy swung long limb from saddle and loped into Dead Crow saloon, SEXiest item of fashion available in opinion of *moi*. V. Baggy grey ones revealing lots of beumbe Etck remain, as they have done since first builder shouted 'Oh wot a luvly pair' from scaffold, least SEXy item in fashion anals.

See also FASHION, TRAINERS.

Builders' Bum Jeans
Bulk Buy

JOBS

Gone are the daze, I am glad to say, when women were supposed to marry houses while men swanned about managing large companies and Doing It with their secretaries (also, digging mines, laying railroads, sewer pipes Etck and other unsavoury jobz we feminists wld like to write out of history, ahem).

But nowadaze both women and men have to slave away to make ends meet and unless they are DINKIES (Dual Income No Kids) they are probably paupers. Either you have several Jobz at once and no time for your family (who are therefore all on streets, hooligans, junkies Etck) or you have NO job and no money for your family (who are therefore all on streets, hooligans, junkies Etck).

174

Teenage Worriers keen to avoid being hooligans, on drugs, streets Etck or becoming parents of same need to develop LIFE-strategy-stuff NOW.

Do all the usual exam stuff which qualifies you to apply for Jobz Etck. When you have put off evil day for as long as you can, you have to apply for a Job. Ideally, you shld know how to spel (ho ho yeech).

JOB SEEKER'S TIP:
Write 6 letters for every vacancy using several aliases and all your relatives' addresses. This may give you a chance of an interview . . .

JOB FACTS:

In Little Britain, under-13s are not allowed Jobz (even part-time ones) legally, so the only option is to work casually for frendz, neighbours Etck. Obvious stuff is car-washing, lawn-mowing, dog-walking. V. Little skill needed (except for not getting windscreens all smeary) but do not confuse and start mowing dog or walking car (joy-riding seriously illegal). Some people suggest baby-sitting, but if you are under 13 you shld still need a baby-sitter yourself and anyway you are not yet the magical age to qualify as a True Teenage Worrier.

Once you ARE a Teenage Worrier, you're allowed to werk part time (not more than two hours on a skule day) but you can't start before 7 a.m.

You're not allowed to do manual work (lifting heavy stuff or working with dangerous machines) until you're 16 and you can't work on the streets (busking, selling stuff) until you're 18. As you can see from under-age prostitutes, this law is badly enforced.

Wages are usually rubbish for kids and there is no minimum (not for Adults either at time of writing but hope New Govt might have changed all that by time of you reading this) and if you kick up a fuss it is V. Unlikely that you will keep Job as the employer will get some other keen young person to exploit instead. This is why El Chubb is so V. Keen on Trade Unions, which at least gave the humble werker a little bit of support.

If you're working for a parent these laws are
flexible, which is why you often see tiny kids
helping out in shops and getting V. Good at
adding up.

Easiest job once you're about 15 is baby-sitting as
long as you don't sit ON the baby, and do get the
phone numbers of local doc, casualty, child's
parents, grandparents Etck Etck. I even asked for
the name of all the godparents when I baby-sat last
month. Maybe that's why the parents got home so
early, looking so Worried, and haven't asked me
back.

See also CAREER, MONEY.

I pulled up
LOADS of these
Thorny old weeds for
you, Mrs Prune

KAMA SUTRA

Indispensable Lurve Guide which shows you all the
Lurve-making positions you can imagine (and quite
a few you haven't thought of yet). How they do
those positions is a mystery to *moi*, however. Are
they made of elastic, or what?

KISSING (PART 3)

I have already dealt with this in my first two bukes.
At length. But not long enough for my reader, it
seems, as Teenage Worriers ask me 'How do you
kiss?' Er . . . I haven't had enough practice. There
was the incident where I cut my nose on Brian's
specs. There was Pashione with Daniel that lasted
three minutes. But did I do it well? He ran off with
Aggy.

  I should say that it affected parts of me I didn't
know I had and evoked such thoughts as 'melting

I know so much
about KISSING,
I can do it
with my
eyes shut

furnace and suffusing flames' Etck and it *appeared* to do the same for him. So obviously this kissing thing comes naturally at some point as long as you linger with it. But this LIFE buke is about getting Out in Werld and doing some other thingz so you're not gluming about thinking only of yr beLurved. I wish it werked for me.

LADS

Single blokes are V. Fashionable nowadays, viz: magazines like *Loaded*, *Pissed*, *Fart*, *Grunt* Etck and TV shows about men who try to Do It with anything even distantly resembling a gurl as long as

it doesn't interfere with the taste of their TV
dinners. Adam is a single bloke, of course, but he's
as different from this kind of boy as if he had come
from another planet, groan, glume, sigh Etck.

LANGUAGE

How you talk still has a V. Big effect on how you
are perceived, according to surveys. 'RP' (received
pronunciation or, in El Chubb's dictionary,
Toffspeak) is yer basic BBC voice. If you speak like

that, most British people (however they speak themselves) will think you are more intelligent, trustworthy Etck than if you drop yer aitches where they should be and add them where they hain't (as in calling an 'h' a 'haitch').

It sometimes seems that if you want to Get On, Rule Werld Etck you need either Accent or Attitude (preferably both). However, as L. Chubb, Karl Marx, Plato and other grate philosophers have often been heard to muse, LIFE is full of contradictions and lots of people rise to Top of heaving pile of yumanity without either Accent or Attitude (viz our last Prime Minister).

Brits are V. Bad at learning other people's languages, 'cos we are so snooty about our own lingo being the werld's most popular, since the Americans speak it. Hence we expect everyone to learn it and if we go to France we do daft things like speak English in a French accent and hope they'll understand.

Loads of languages are becoming extinct: there are currently 2,500 languages in the world, but anthropologists reckon that in 23 years' time there may only be 60!! Where will the other 2,440 go to? Rescue a language by learning one today! And why not start with:

LETTIC
How cld I resist putting this in? It is the group of languages spoken by the old Prussians, the Lettish (mainly from Latvia) and Lithuanians. Let's learn it.

LIFE

Let me quote from the *Concise Oxford Dictionary*:
'State of functional activity and continual exchange
peculiar to organized matter, and esp. to the portion
of it constituting animal or plant before banana,
animate existence, being alive . . .'

Yes, fellow Worriers! This is it! This is that great
thingamajig we're experiencing. The Dict does not
say 'banana', by the way, it uses that Other Werd
about dying that rhymes with 'breath'.

But if LIFE only pertains to organized matter
then what am I doing stuck in the middle of it? A
tangled ball of wool is more organized than *moi* –
and it is made of matter, surely. So which of us is
the more alive?

As for functional activity – hmmmm. I s'pose I
perform functions (many of them unmentionable in
a family buke). But do I *have* a function? That is, a
purpose in LIFE? And do I engage in continual
exchange? Argggg.

This causes me to ponder on how little we can
discover of the true yuman meaning of werds by
simply looking them up in the dictionary.

EL CHUBB'S LIFE-TIPS:
  *Now, you've already described what you LOOK
like (see IMAGE section, above). But this is a much
better exercise. Describe YOURSELF. Without *any
reference to your looks at all*. Resist 'tall' or 'black' or

'skinny' or any of that stuff. Think about what your family might like about you. And your frendz. (If no family OR frendz, not even one, then is there anything the social worker might appreciate, or the goldfish?) Try describing someone else in your LIFE this way:

'Very little conversation, but restful personality. Never argues.' If I add 'Appears to enjoy swimming in circles' you will see that I am describing a goldfish. But the latter remark is based on a rather low choice-threshold for a fish in a bowl . . . You shld find it easier describing a dog or cat, and easier still describing a person. Think *character*.

*GET OUT THERE! The best antidote to Worrying about Yrself and how you look/seem/are is to do something in the werld that helps you forget. If you only hang out with other Worriers examining yr spots, lanky wigs Etck (you must do *some* of this, as you know by now) you are bound to pine.

But if you go to films, clubs, get into team sports, hobbies, music Etck Etck then the werld opens up and you find you have something else to Worry about (like whether you have perfect pitch, can draw like da Vinci Etck), which is a whole lot better than worrying about yr Image.

*ACCEPT YRSELF. There are bits you like, bits you don't. Same is true of every person on the planet. You're only a Yuman Bean, and there's only so much a Yuman Bean can do (am I stringing you along? Ha ha yeeech).

*DON'T LISTEN TO HORRIBLE PEOPLE:
'Sticks and stones may break my bones but words
will never hurt me.'

There never was a more *un*-true rhyme in the
world. But let's make it come true. Anyone who says
anything mean about the way you look (or the way
anyone else looks) just isn't worth bothering about.

*ER, THINK POSITIVE: Ahem, as you know,
El Chubb is not always V. Good at this. Worrying is
not best route to Positive Thinking. But a handy tip
wld be to look at the descriptions you gave above of
the way you ARE. Then change any negative
descriptions either to positive ones or to neutral
ones, eg (I'll take a *looks* example): 'I have a vast,
hideous nose' could become 'My hooter is like a
Roman Emperor's', or 'On the Richter scale of noses,
mine would be high', or 'Thank God, I've got a
nose. What would I pick otherwise?' or 'I love my
nose! Without it, how would I smell?' (No old jokes
per-*lease*.)

By working this krafty Positive Thinking stuff, a
speechlessly shy person can become enigmatic, a
Crazed Worrier is transformed into conscientious
and caring, a bossy-boots becomes full of leadership
potential Etck Etck. NB If you've only written nice
thingz about yourself in the first place you are not a
Worrier (tell me how you do it).

*DO GREAT WORKS: The Best People in the
werld did not do stuff because of what they looked
like but because of who they were. They used talents

to invent, change, campaign, make, build, paint, describe, analyse, dissect Etck Etck all the brilliant things on the planet. Only models and film stars rely on their looks. That is considerably less than 1% of the population, so why are we hung up on them? Is it 'cos we think no-one will Lurve us unless we're beautiful? But is that why we Lurve our frendz?

Teenage Worriers considering Grate Werks

LUXURY

Luxury is not just for the rich. Luxury is for You and Me, dearest Worriers. You do not need to sun yrself in foreign climes, bathe in champagne or ride wild white horses through the surf (nobody needs this, naturally, but a small amount of yearning is allowed): you can get DIY Luxury on tap at home, if only you organize yrself.

Luxury
Is two bags of fudge.

Luxury
Is Rover and a hot water bottle. Rover makes me sneeze, the HWB is leaky, but the moment of Luxury before the sneezing and the damp is worth it, oh Yes!

Luxury
Is curling up with Rover, fudge, hot water bottle, blanket, TV, Music, V.Good buke and being brought a cup of hot chocolate by my only mother. This happens when moon is blue, but I am even prepared to make my own Hot choccy in order to experience this remarkable glow.

Luxury

Is when the bath water runs hot (about twice a week in our house) and there is a half centimetre of Jumbo Bubblo left in Benjy's bubble bath. (My mother locks hers away, and benjy's, being V.Cheap, gives me eczema....but who cares?) For ten mins, until water is tepid. I can lie in scalding foam imagining I am Queen of Persia Etck.

Luxury

Is when there are three good programmes on the TV, it is pouring with rain outside and the heating's working (see bath, above).

Fudge de-Luxe

CHAPTER EIGHT
MMMMMMze to OOOOOOOze

Oh, glorious Saturday morn . . .

I arrived on time, flushed yet serene. V. Worried to find that none of the films showing were called Large Door and immediately experienced familiar sinking feeling as though lead weight were pulling me into Jurassic Swamp. Had I

a) Gone to wrong cinema?

b) Been stood up?

c) Been victim of grisly hoax whereby a load of Adam's mates would jump out from behind a pillar jeering?

Oh me of little faith! There he was: a vision of flowing wig (gleaming midnight spirals . . .) and lissom limbs loping towards me, waving tickets for L'Âge d'Or (French, of course). Don't ask me about the film. I was aware only of Adam's smouldering presence (of course it was a No Smoking cinema, you fuel) and the intense anticipation of the KISS. In fact, he was rather absorbed by the film and, er, did not, sadly, do more than run his fingers shatteringly through my wig Etck until later . . .

How is it possible to concentrate under such circumstances? Nevertheless, I bluffed my way interllekshually through the content of L'Âge d'Or, amid the sweet nothings we exchanged afterwards, over a stale chikko-burger and a flat Coke. We talked of everything in the werld. My life has been a pale shadow of an existence till now. We are going to continue with the film course to get as much as we can from it and to pursue our projects despite Sleeve, then we will set up our own film company: Lettadam. (The name may need some fine tuning but is better, we thought, than Chubbstone.) There are loads of places that will give us dosh, he sez – organizations for Young Film Makers Etck Etck and maybe we could even write to Mogul. Yes! Adam believes in miracles! And so do I! Together we can do it. Together. Together . . .

Now that I have been wined and dined (coked and burgered sounds a trifle rude) by Adam Stone, Wyoming-Grilled Chikko will never seem the same . . . it is true what they say about Lurve – it flourishes against the odds.

What cared we for the dog poo that we slid in? What cared we for the abusive winos to whom we scattered our few precious remaining coins? Or for the litter that flapped against our thighs as we ambled through the mean streets in the driving rain, entwined in our mutual dream?

When Adam laughed, the rain glistened on his sculptèd brow just like in the movies and then, just like in the movies, he clasped me to his manly chest and . . . kissed me.

Throb. Pulse. Meltdown.

Alas, we cannot meet over the weekend as he has to go to visit a sick aunt in Kent (had never realized how many sick relatives there are in the werld before), but I will see him on Thursday at the course and we will make another date then!

My happiness knows no bounds. I yam a woooman who has kissed ecstatically, Etck.

Today, I shall laze and dream and devote myself to plans for Lettadam . . . Chubbadam . . . Lettystone *. . . in which our talents will mingle and combine to surge forth and float to New Horizons on wings of Art . . .*

ARG. *You won't* believe *what has just happened.*

I was shuffling dreamily downstairs (having wallowed in ecstatic memories of last night and re-read above diary entry 6 times, wondering how better to describe my rapture) when I glimpsed a letter on the door mat. For moi.

Letty, Letty, Letty!

My heart is breaking. I know you can never forgive me, nor do I expect you to, but last night I saw you kissing Adam Stone and I cannot bear for you to be hurt again, my own, my dearest sensitive flower!

Stone is two-timing you with that babe from LA.

I don't know if I should tell you this but when I saw you with another I knew what I should have known long, long ago. That I love you, have always loved you. Dare I say it, WILL always love you!

Of course I expect nothing from you, except, perhaps, that you will allow me from time to time to take tea with you, just to be near you, and perhaps, one day, to take you to the theatre before you are married and whisked away from me for evermore.

All I do beg is that you find someone who will cherish you as I should have done and that you are not deceived by Adam Stone, who has broken hearts from here to Iceland (where his nature truly resides) and back.

If, by the smallest, tiniest, flimsiest, minutest chance, you wish to see me again, just to tell me you forgive me, I shall wait for you on Thursday after your Film Course. If you come out with Adam Stone, I shall know all is lost. If not, I'll see you by the bench round the corner (you remember the one — how could I forget!) where first we declared our love.

Forever yours,

Daniel.

Argggggggg.

Adam Stone two timing me? Never!

But is that really an aunt he's visiting?

And what of Candice? Has she really gone back to LA or is she in fact in KENT?

The seeds of doubt are sown. Despair descends, gripping me in icy grip.

MANNERS

What do you say?

Your money or your LIFE

please

Manners used to be something you had to learn from etiquette bukes if you wanted to make it in a thing called 'Society'. For instance, a Real Lady would be someone who treats a duke and a dustman just the same. I wld certainly qualify as a Real Lady under this definition, if I knew any dukes. You can probably use a few rools even in today's don't-care-trample-on-a-pensioner-before-breakfast world: Not farting and picking hooter in company, frinstance.

MODELS

See SUPERMODELS.

£ **MONEY** £ £ £ £ £ £ £

Q: *What is the worst way to spend a million pounds?*
(Think before you read the answer, as it is a V. Big
insight of El Chubb's, and you won't get it unless
you think. Have you thought? Go on, think again.
I'll print the answer rather small so you don't see it
until you've had a serious thought . . .)

A: *Give 50p to two million people.*

Arg. See? V. Worrying, espesh, for *moi* who is a
socialist. But as you see, it is necessary to share, but
wisely.

s'all I get
paid, so s'all
I'll sell

peanuts

↑ <u>NB</u> wonder
what sign
Euro-currency will be?

In order for us Teenage Worriers to enjoy the rest
of our lives, we will need Money. But how much?
Obviously if we're honest, a whole lot doesn't help
that much, but it is better than none. What we
NEED is to know we can have enough, and that is
what the Govt over the last 15 years or so has tried
to stop people hoping and believing. So everyone has
been trying to make as much as possible in order to
stash some away for rainy days, redundancies Etck
Etck. El Chubb thinks the most Imp campaign of
all is for real Social Security. Then people wld be
happy to werk in decent caring professions like
teaching, doctoring, social werk Etck and not feel
failures 'cos they don't get free lunches, expense
accounts Etck Etck and not fear that they might be
laid off anyway.

In the meantime, there are some ways round
having no dosh (which is the eternal state of the
Teenage Worrier).

1) *Swap stuff*: Your frendz' bukes, tapes, clothes
Etck may be boring to them and fascinating to you.
You may even have something *they* want. Then swap
it. You cld swap it for a month even, or for ever.

2) *Presents*: Instead of whingeing on about
horrible things you've been given, how about
making sure you get what you want at Christmas
and birthdays? Ask for tokens or money, or for every
Adult you know to band together for those
astronomically expensive roller-blades Etck.

Exploit the younger generation...

3) *Save*: In order to save, you got to have something in the first place and in Hard Times like these there are Teenage Worriers who don't get anything at all. My Adored Father didn't even get a bus fare when he was a kid and had to walk 6 miles to skule as he never fails to remind *moi*. We all want a lot of stuff these days and we have to earn or save to get it rather than badger our poor old folks.

4) *Car Boot Sales*: Not bad for picking up bargains, prezzies Etck, also grate for getting rid of your parents' CDs Etck (just a joke). Snag is, you need a car, so co-operation from elder generation usually necessary.

5) *Get a Job*: There is a limit on what you are allowed to do until you're 18 (see JOBS) but here are a few tips until I get round to writing my major opus (Latin for Grate Werk) entitled

Unless you give impression of being able to clean and grrom yrself, you may draw a blank...

FIVE THOUSAND WAYS TO EARN 50P:
* START A SERVICE: Instead of banging
hopelessly on doors only to be faced by disgruntled
residents complaining that you are ruining their
Sunday snooze, why not put cards through their
doors advertising yourself? i.e.: V. GOOD CAR-
WASHING/DOG-WALKING/PET-GROOMING/
WEEDING BY EXPERTS; BRILLIANT
DECORATING BY ZAK AND ZIP. Make *sure* a
sensible adult has checked out where you are going
to werk and that you *never* go into a strange house
alone!!!!! There's a lot of odd jobs you can do that
adults would prefer not to do and if you do them
really well you'll be asked back.

Also, you can swap a service for a service – ie:
offer to sweep up in the hairdresser's for a free
haircut, muck out riding stables for a free ride Etck.
*MAKE STUFF: You can sell hand-made cards to
local shops or any of your hobby-type stuff (see
HOBBIES) and even do a sign that goes with them:
HANDCRAFTED BY LOCAL TEENAGE
WORRIER, frinstance.

As any Worried Cynic knows by now, this is
unlikely to make your fortune. But it's worth
remembering that the V. Posh Department Store in
London, Horrids, started LIFE as a fruit & veg stall
in a market.

BARGAIN EMPORIUM

Cheap'n'cheerful prezzies for the whole family for under a fiver each!

Roll of sticky Tape!
Barely used!!

"BALL-O-WOOL"

UNUSUAL SOCKS
Barely matching!
Seldom used!

Nearly new FORK.

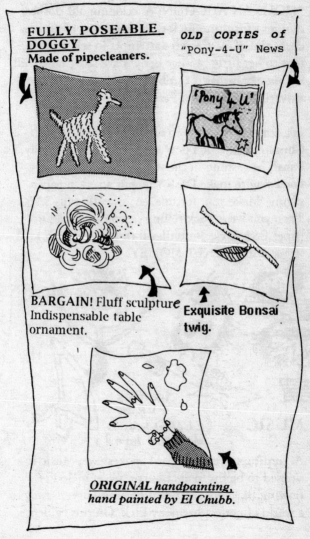

FULLY POSEABLE DOGGY
Made of pipecleaners.

OLD COPIES of "Pony-4-U" News

BARGAIN! Fluff sculpture
Indispensable table
ornament.

Exquisite Bonsai twig.

ORIGINAL handpainting,
hand painted by El Chubb.

*HOLD AN AUCTION: Auctioning old clothes, mother's furniture Etck is V. Good way of raising dosh, though L. Chubb's attempts to sell his own toys to her little brother Benjy have sadly failed: all the money he has is cardboard coins from his new Privatized Postperson Patricia Playset.

For other 4,997 ways to earn 50p send SAE to L. Chubb, kreator of Yuniverse. Do not expect reply, as I shall be cashing in the stamps. (This is actually good way to make Dosh — ie: put an ad in paper saying 'Make your fortune, enclose 50p plus SAE'. Then you write back telling person to put ad in paper Etck Etck. Prob illegal though, whinge.)

See also POCKET MONEY.

MUSIC

THE NICE GURLS (El chubb's dream band)

According to ye grate Bard Spokeshave, Music is s'posed to be the food of Lurve, sweet melodies flowing like crystal streams bearing Lurvers away to a world of perfect harmony Etck. On this evidence,

Spokeshave had clearly not visited the Toxic Rat Klub in Werld's End Lane recently, because the Music there makes you feel as if you've been trapped inside a washing-machine.

Let me say, dear student of LettyLIFE, I am a big fan of all kinds of Music, because I do think that it reaches the parts other creative stuff doesn't reach, including admittedly some parts (ahem, wince, tingle, twitch) that the Guardians of Our Souls are always flapping about when they moan that all Pop Music other than Cliff Richard represents Catastrophic Moral Decline Etck (and if they only like Cliff Richard then they could be in favour of Catastrophic *Mental* Decline anyway). Music is about the Whole Person, it seems to *moi*, body and mind together, and that's why it has such a big effect on us, and espesh on Teenage Worriers whose bodies and minds are entwined in such an intense way, chance would be a fine thing, moan, whinge Etck.

There are many musical tastes in the Chubb household. Adored Mother thinks Mozart is like the quality of light in summer, Beethoven like the fearful restlessness of the elements, the Bee Gees like the kind of men she wished Adored Father had been, nice arty white suits and long hair, Sensitive Feelings, voices like choirboys Etck. She recently asked me if Underground, Garage, Jungle, or House were new forms of Teenage Habitat . . . Adored Father has big collection of Heavy Metal records,

Rover's love song...

but when pressed admits he can't remember any of
the songs, due to chemically induced confusion
when originally experiencing same. Benjy likes
banging a tin tray on the side of his head whilst
attempting to play 'Frère Jacques' on the recorder
one-handed.

For *moi*self, I like old Art Skule rock (Sonic Beaver Etck) because it sounds like bedraggled, intense types trying to make sense of an alien world (like *moi*), some dance music, old Brit classical composers like Elgar and Vaughan Williams who make me cry and want to be a horse, and some of Ashley's jazz records, even if they do sound a bit like people doing algebra out loud. Music is the food of LIFE, sez *moi*, and if things go on the way they are it might be the closest to pashione I'm going to get, sniff, whinge, cower, suck thumb for want of better things (a message from the Moral Decline of the Nation Dept), mope, kick Etck Etck.

Learning a Musical Instrument, however, is one of LIFE's grate Joyz, I have observed from those of my frendz lucky enough to have

a) Thought of it themselves
b) Been made to do it by their parents
c) Had enough dosh for lessons.

Teenage Worriers in Sluggs orchestra always seem somewhat Less Worried than the rest of us. Playing Music seems to have given Meaning to their LIFE.

Surveys now seem to suggest that learning about Music early is good for all other kinds of learning (also good for soul Etck). But the Govt doesn't seem V. Interested and is busy cutting Music Teachers from Primary Skules wherever poss.

I didn't even get to play recorder, though I am glad to (or sad to) say Benjy now has opp of learning this for free and I think I can stand the noise as long as it keeps him from Worrying about floors for a few more moments. I wish I had learned

1) Piano
2) Cello
3) Saxophone
4) Double Bass.

But I have finally gathered up ye courage to ask Sluggs Music Dept if I can learn Accordion!! My reasons are: no-one else at skule plays it, so I can't be compared to anyone; and also, the piano teacher told me she has one and wld Lurve to teach someone. Hold your breath for Letty Chubb, great Accordionist. I can see self now, in French beret Etck.

See also CLUBS.

The accordion is sad and happy at once, like <u>moi</u>

N AMES

Those of us struggling under burdens like Scarlett (a result of my selfish Mother's obsession with *Gone with the Wind*) need solace when it comes to the

count your blessings dept.

name business. I am hoping to get Adam to call me Diana, as in proud, goddess-like creature, and our offspring will be David and Daisy, enabling us to live in 4D (four dimensions, so there) without having to time travel.

NAPALM

Q: *Should you drop a jellied petrol made from thickening agent made from naphthalene and coconut oil on to babies when you know that it will burn their skin off?*
A: *Not really, but we did.*

Well, the Americans did in the Vietnam War.

I put this in because it's clear that individual

American Teenage Worriers (the average age of the soldiers who fought the war was 19) would have answered 'No' to the above question. But they did it anyway, as a group, and under orders.

EL CHUBB's LIFE-TIP: Question orders. Question causes. Question Big Ideas. You could seem to be the lone voice against dictatorship. But where there's one voice, others will follow.

NATURAL ✤

The use of this werd in ads for cosmetics Etck has always amused Yrs Truely vastly. You can spend a LIFEtime achieving that Nachural look. I am still offering El Chubb's Vampire (I mean Vamp) make-up kit to anyone who sends me a cosmetic ad without the word Nachural in it.

However, being Nachural in LIFE shld mean being yourself, which has to be a pretty Good Thing to be. I have tried V. Hard to be someone else for large chunks of my short-ish existence but I always end up being me in the end and wonder why I bothered. We're not talking about the way you LOOK here, although leaving yourself pretty much as you are seems V. Reasonable to *moi*, but the way you act and feel and talk and move.

People are always trying to improve themselves. But who for? Their parents? Their bosses? Their Teachers? Some Lurve-Object? OR an Almighty

Butch likes ballet

Sylvie rollerblades to Mozart

L. Chubb Motto (No. 2468):

Bernice
bonds with
hedgehogs

Cuthbert collects
cat postacrds

Rover ponders nature
by Mouse mousse

BE YOURSELF

Being who is looking down from on high and saying, 'You SLOUCH. Stand UP!'

or 'Have you seen the state of your wig/hairbrush/room?'

or 'We Godz hate freckles and you won't get into heaven wearing an anorak.'

Going for what YOU find interesting is the key to a good LIFE and to know what that is, you need to know who you ARE. So knowing your Nachural Self is a V. Good thing to start with.

Here are some ways:

1) Think about what you LIKE. Not what is fashionable. You might really like Elgar's Cello Concerto better than Bean and the Maggots (currently Number One, in case you didn't know) but be too ashamed to admit it, even to YOURSELF. See how daft that is?

2) Wear the colours you like. Yes! Even beige! (Just don't expect me to talk to you.)

3) If you like reading *Thrills & Swoon* you are allowed. Just 'cos I can't get past the first page of those bukes without throwing up, it doesn't matter.

4) If you want to dance all night and snort Coke . . . don't. Knowing who you are means knowing how to take care of who you are. Doing illegal stuff is not taking care of yourself. Hurting other people's feelings isn't either.

If you pretend to be different in order to catch a

Lurver or make a frend, then they'll find you out sooner or later or else you'll be pretending all your LIFE.

RULES OF DECORUM FORBID:
* Total lack of washing.
* Farting, nose-picking Etck in company (though see nose-picking for campaign against this foolish prejudice).
* Saying exactly what you think, when you think it. Think it, but don't always say it. It could hurt someone else.
* Physical or mental violence.
* Public nudity. (Don't really understand this rule, either, though it wouldn't suit *moi* as I need four layers at least until June, then back on again in Sept.)

<u>Avoid</u> <u>Nudity</u> <u>with</u> <u>El</u> <u>Chubb</u>

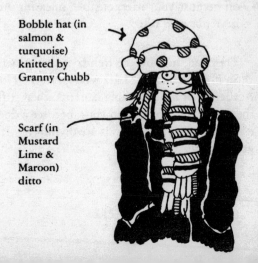

Bobble hat (in salmon & turquoise) knitted by Granny Chubb

Scarf (in Mustard Lime & Maroon) ditto

NEIGHBOURS

V.V.V. Imp to like your neighbours if at all poss and also to avoid watching the TV programme of the same name as scientists employed by L. Chubb have revealed brain damage resulting from prolonged exposure to same.

REASONS TO LIKE NEIGHBOURS:

* They will have spare set of keys for those many occasions on which you have lost yours.
* They will let you sit by their radiator when you have ice inside your windows.
* They will give you thimbleful of milk, sugar Etck which your Mother is so V. Bad at remembering to buy.
* They MAY even let you use their phone (as long as you have appropriate dosh) when yours is cut off because your irresponsible, uncaring Adults have not paid bill.

They can, in short, be frendz against cruel werld. So if you hate their kidz who go to the Nobs Academy, or have horrible haircuts, then stifle it. If their window box falls on your foot, see a doc but don't sue. Neighbourhoods are dwindling. If you've got one, treasure it.

NITS

You know what these are. Call them pendiculosis, if you prefer. If you've never had them, tell me your secret, as London Skules are their favourite nesting place (or rather the wigs of the unfortunate inhabitants). Some people still think it is a sign of dirtiness to have nits. Not so. They don't care if your hair is dirty *OR* squeaky clean; they simply jump skittishly from wig to wig in an completely indiscriminate manner and do not know if you're a Nice Person or not.

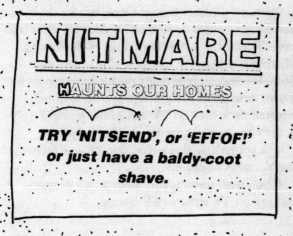

NITMARE

HAUNTS OUR HOMES

TRY 'NITSEND', or 'EFFOF!'
or just have a baldy-coot
shave.

The only sensible way to get rid of these little blighters is to comb hair regularly with a fine-tooth comb. Lotions and potions contain chemicals and have to be used on a rotational basis anyway as the Super-nits of today have become resistant to them.

METHOD: Wash wig; dollop on *loads* of conditioner; comb carefully with V. fine-tooth comb (you can get them from chemist; metal ones are best) over a bit of kitchen roll. If any Nits emerge, then repeat process every three days for a couple of weeks. And enjoy a Nit-free LIFE (or at least a few Nit-free weeks). Arg.

NOSE-PICKING

Underrated pleasure thought repellent by those who haven't discovered its joys and hidden by those who have. This is the last guilty refuge of the Teenage Worrier but begs the question of manners, morals Etck. Frinstance, how many people have you seen mown down, slaughtered, decimated, tortured, violated Etck Etck on TV and in the movies? And how many have you seen picking their noses?

Ask yourself: is this a true, fair, or sane picture of the Yuman Condition?

If you wish to complain about a lack of nose-picking on TV write to TV bosses.

NUCLEAR POWER/ENERGY

V. Big Worry for all Yoof as this source of energy

still dominates our lives and one small mistake can result in a Chernobyl (the Russian nuclear station that hit meltdown and killed a lot of people and wrecked the surroundings). Current ways of getting rid of nuclear waste seem unsatisfactory. This is an understatement.

To campaign for Safe Energy, join an environmental group.

NUNS

What I will become if LIFE goes wrong. Sigh.

OLD AGE

In my exhaustive surveys about what Teenage Worriers Worry most about, I found that pensions (surprise, surprise) come V. Low on the list. But it is my job to edukate, instrukt Etck. So here is a little lecture:

1) Old People sometimes sound like Boring Old Twits who go on about the same things over and over, forget they told you the thing they're telling you five minutes ago, complain about Yr Manners/Hair/Clothes/Language/Music Etck Etck. Sometimes they do this because they really are Old

Twits, but those are prob also the people who were Young Twits first and just haven't changed much. The others are qu. likely doing it because most of the people they know, including their own offspring and the Teenage Worriers that have ishooed therefrom, don't bother to listen to them, so they just keep repeating it in the hope that eventually someone will hear, like shipwrecked sailors throwing lots of bottles with notes in into the ocean.

2) Old People need decent pensions. They were young once. You will be old one day. They fought wars, werked hard, blah blah to look after offspring, defend democracy Etck, and are now on scrap heap of poverty. Worry about them now and it will make V. Big Diff to whether or not you are condemned to become an Old Age Worrier yrself.

OMELETTE

If you learn nothing else from this humble tome, you can at least learn simple cooking. Then you can convince parent this is worthwhile buke.

Put a very little (VERY little – *very very* little) butter in non-stick pan. Get it V. Hot. Break two eggz into mixing bowl. Stir them up and add a pinch of salt. Pour eggz into pan so they look nice and flat like pancake. Get fish slice and *as soon as* edge of egg looks stiffish, lift it up, tilt pan so that runny egg goes under stiff bit. Continue until it's

JUST not runny. If you go on any more, it gets like plasterboard. Take omelette out of pan. Eat. If desired, start off by browning chopped onions, bacon, peppers, ham, other goodies and by grating cheese into eggz. Add eggz to other stuff and cook as above.

Most Teenage Worriers don't know how to make an omelette. That's because our lousy parents just take a fish finger out of the ice compartment and stick it in a pan. If only they taught us gourmet cooking *à la Chubb* we wld be much healthier.

OMENS

XYZ Files, Paranormal stuff Etck has been all the rage for a while on TV but they are qu. bad for superstitious Teenage Worriers in the humble opinion of L. Chubb. We have enough to Worry about, wot with black cats, ladders, months with '13' in them Etck Etck. I prefer not to lie awake wondering if Zolga the Nerd is about to materialize in my bedroom and whisk me off for SEX-experiments Etck.

Whoooooooooo oooO

↖ wind

Blinding flash ✦

↖ Lightning, or electricity
On blink

SCREECH

↖ You have trodden on
cat's tail

Horrible squeaks

↖ did you oil your
bike?

El Chubb's pocket guide to Things-that-go-Bump-in-the-Night.

219

CHAPTER NINE
PPPPPPEEEEEEze

But wait, what light through yonder winder gleams?
Adam Stone has betrayed me, woe and glume

BUT

Daniel Hope loves me still.
Can it be true? I am awash with emotion as the iceberg
of my heart softens, melts, cascades into a flood of
longing . . .
I had turned my back on him, knowing he would never
Be Mine. How faithless I have been, to think of Another
when obviously Daniel's relationship with Sarah Spiggott
was profoundly superficial and he was yearning for me all
along.
At long last, he has seen the error of his ways and
realized where his true Lurve lies.
Adam Stone already seems just a blip in the steady
graph of my eternal Lurve for D. Hope, now honed on the
furnace of adversity Etck Etck.
There is no doubt in my heart. I shall fly to the bench
immediatement (well, on Thursday after class anyway)
and swear unswerving devotion to Daniel.
Meanwhile I shall enjoy going on film course tomorrow
and ignoring Adam Stone. Heh! heh! Mad cackle of
triumph Etck.

*Must admit to Worry over Father, whose glume deepens as
each day passes with no news of his buke. Has it really
sunk without trace? Is fiction as fickle as fact? Is the
world of bukes as unpredictable as the world of Un-true
Lurve?*

*If only my Adored Father had turned his talents to the
micro-chipo like boring Neville then we could be
champagne socialists and my Mother wld never look at
Another. Glume, despond.*

THURSDAY:
*V. Interesting film course today. Sleeve has finally woken
up to my talent, rolled himself up Etck and has paid teensy
fee of £5 to option my pix of Aggy and siblings for further
use. Meanwhile I am developing film storyboard re
Granny Chubb, which he says is 'V. Promising'. Preen
Etck. (Wait till he sees my video of a London street
overflowing with crime, grime, corruption Etck.) Moiself
overflowing with new-found confidence re Daniel. I barely
noticed Adam Stone except to think he looked somewhat on
the lanky side and that his hair was more greasy than
shiny. I contrived to step on his foot, however, as I left.*

*He ran down the stairs after me and grabbed me
roughly by the arm. How dare he? I shrugged him off.
(Have read about people shrugging Despised Ones off in
bukes, and it is easier than you think, even with shoulders
like mine.)*

'What's up?' he queried with startling originality.

*'Nothing whatsoever,' I swiftly replied with rapier-like
wit, sarcasm Etck. 'Hope you had a lovely time in Kent.'*

And added as a parting shot, 'With Candice.'

Fled into night, pausing only to notice a look of bewilderment on Adam's face – the face I once thought dear. But where his image was, now shines only Daniel . . . who even now I fly to meet . . .

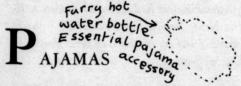

PAJAMAS

Have just discovered you can spell pyjamas this way too. What to wear to bed is a Big Worry for *moi*, as I hate those dinky nightie thingz with pink teddies or bows on but I can't qu. bring myself to wear the boyz stuff either, which is usually covered in super heroes or American baseball logos. I need a nice stripy nightshirt made of V. Warm stuff. Or plain red pyjamas. If you have a pair, cld you write in and tell me where you got them? Meanwhile, I recommend my current suave style of four of Only Father's old T-shirts and a jumper.

PANDORA

Famous character of Greek myth. She was a Naughty Gurl who opened a box she wasn't supposed to open. Out flew every horrible thing in the world: Pestilence, Famine, Plague, Glume, Dume Etck Etck. So these things weren't here

before? Come *on*. Pull the other one. But a
'Pandora's Box' has come to mean something you
shouldn't delve into . . . and there are such things, of
course, like secrets that someone else is guarding.
One good thing about the Pandora story is that she
didn't move fast enough to get the lid back on in
time to stop the last little thing fluttering out of the
box. That little thing was HOPE. And it flutters
round still, guarding us from despair for eternity.

PARENTS

NB True, even if you've never met them

You can't help having Parents, though they cld have
helped having you, which is the source of a famous
cry of the desperate Teenage Worrier, 'I never asked
you to have me in the first place.' One of the
massive Probs of LIFE that has to be faced is that
Teenage Worriers have at some time in our Teenage
Worrying years to stand up to our Parents and
Become Ourselves, and Adored Parents have to
realize this has got to happen, and not fight against
it. Sometimes, of course, we may be headed on V.
Self-Destructive course that Lurving Parents are
morally obliged to try to guide us away from, but
some time between their own Wild Yoof of Doing
It, Abusing Bod With Dodgy Thingz Etck and
becoming Responsible Citizens many Parents
unfortunately lose the ability to distinguish between
the normal Luny Behaviour of The Young, and the

You better believe it

Parents, part 2864

conviction that their beLurved Ickle Babas have fallen into the hands of Drug Fiends, Slave-Traders, Group SEX Cults Etck. This can affect the judgement of Parents: we have to Deal With this, and whether we have to Deal With It kindly or unkindly can be to do with how bad their judgement has become.

But I also have a Thought of Chairman Chubb: most Parents, except for V. Crazed Ones, want nothing more from their children than that they should be Happy. Their idea of Happiness may be different from ours sometimes, but that doesn't matter. They also have to deal with V. Diff psychological thingz like seeing us grow into clever, desirable (chance wld be a fine thing, sniff, grump, moan), energetic beingz with good memories Etck, who don't get puffed running upstairs, just at the time of LIFE when they're having trouble with all these thingz themselves. Bear this in mind before calling Adored Parents Uncaring, Hateful, Interfering Stupid Scumbags, O Fellow Teenage Worriers. It will all happen to us one day. NB If I could only follow own rools, wot a haven of sweetness and light our little hovel wld become . . .

PARTIES AR 999

Although Tragick LIFE-Worries like whether I'll be mistaken for a twiglet prevent *moi* from attending more than one party every decade or so I believe it is V. Imp for Teenage Worriers to celebrate LIFE at all opportunities. It helps events to stand out from the usual Mists of Glume, and gives you Memories to Treasure Etck. The rich tapestry Etck is throbbing with Special Moments if only we can seek them out. NB Celebration Parties can be V. cheap and the best thing is, YOU are in control. Viz: Get everyone to bring pack of crisps and V. Unhealthy drink. All you have to do is provide hovel.

EL CHUBBO'S LIST OF THINGZ TO CELEBRATE

1) Day you learnt to walk (probably, like me, you have no idea which day this was, but *some* people's adoring parents keep baby bukes with these cutesy details in and you may as well make some use of them that isn't nauseatingly embarrassing). Ditto first smile, tooth Etck. If not blessed with Lurving family who bothered to write such thingz down (MY family certainly didn't), then celebrate fact you ever learnt to walk at all! Think how V. Hard this was to do. You only have to watch toddling infants tripping over bits of fluff, crashing to floor, wailing piteously, hauling selves up only to soldier on and hurtle to floor again to see what incredible determination this task takes. If only we cld apply such effort to all the tasks of LIFE the werld wld be a Better Place. As for learning to talk! It takes just

three years! How come Sluggs Comprehensive can't teach us French then?

2) Your first period! Radical! (I know some of you are still waiting – I waited long enough, and if you are a boy you shld be prepared to wait as long as possible, ie: Ever. How about a voice-breaking party for you? Squeeeeak, grunt.)

3) If you add on ALL your family's weddings, b'days, new jobs, redundancies Etck you cld have a

party every week of the year. Think of how it will be in 30 years' time when your own simpering offspring ask: "Where did 'ooo an' dada meet?" And you reply: 'At the birthday party for my best frend'z tortoise's daughter.'

PARTY-WORRIER'S TIPS:
* Go with frend if poss. This helps you get in the door without fainting and may give you someone to talk to (until frend is whisked away by wunderbabe into snogging corner leaving you glumier than before).
* Wear something V.V. Simple, pref in shade of Ebony or Fog. Christmas tree balls on ears OK for Christmas. Also V. Comfy for quick getaway. No glass slippers.
* Eat before you go. This will soak up any stray alcohol you may mistakenly imbibe (ahem) and will compensate for V. Unpleasant snacks to be found at most parties, ie: cheesy wotnots mixed with fag ash, 'French' bread with consistency of iron bar Etck.

Kool 'Hint of Midnight' Designer Top.

Kool 'Touch of Cave' Joggers

Moi: enjoying a party

* Remove food from face, teeth Etck before entering party venue, unless you want to be that person with the special peanut butter and spinach smile.

Arg. How is humble *moi* to give this kind of advice when I always end up hiding in loo, under pile of coats Etck? Go to cinema instead.

PERIOD

Your Periods will start sometime between the ages of 10 and 17. If you haven't started at 16 and are also exhibiting no other signs of puberty (eg: body hair, bazooms), get a doctor to check it out.

Irregular Periods are V.V. Common, particularly early on in yr cycle, so don't fret if you have a Period and then don't have one for several months. It takes a while for them to get going. Once Periods have really got started, they go on. And on. Dum-di-dum. Roughly every 28 days. Tra-la-la. Whatever you do. Dum-di-dum. This is a Fact of LIFE and shld not be regarded as a matter of glume, dume Etck as most Teenage Worriers will not get particularly bad cramps or particularly bad PMT (Pre Menstrual Tension). Those who do, however, shld retire with vast hot water bottles and weep for three days. There are still mothers who think their daughters shouldn't swim, have nookie Etck while

I'm wearing **TWO** winged panty-liners. And I still can't catch a ball...

they have a Period. There may be V. Good reasons for abstaining from activities – eg: sloth, disinclination – but, unless you are one of unlucky few with V.V. Bad Periods, menstruation is not one of them. And, as a Proudly-Slothful Worrier, I hate to admit it, but exercise is sometimes the best thing for cramps, as it increases blood flow and stops clots and therefore stops cramps (which is your trusty bod trying to expel clots). Hey-ho. One note of glume, however. If you *do* have V.V. bad pains, it could be worth seeing yr doc, just in case it *is* a sign of something wrong (like endometriosis). Aargh! Worry, worry.

You can, in fact, do anything you like when you have a period but you also must wear towels or tampons. Some Teenage Worriers are scared of tampons 'cos they think they might disappear up inside. Not possible. The vaginal passage is completely closed by the neck of the womb (cervix), so once you've put a tampon in, it can only come out one way. However, it IS possible to forget tampons are there and this can lead to infection or even Toxic Shock, which is V. Dangerous. It's better to use the new whizzo shaped towels (despite nauseating ad for wings Etck) when you can. Never use tampons that are more absorbent than you need for your flow (do NOT be that gurl who bungs in a super-plus in case she comes on) and don't leave them in overnight. You can always use pads then.

El Chubb's Campaign for Embarrassment-Free Periods is gaining support. A large sculpture made of pads, towels, tampons through the ages is to be erected in Sluggs playground next term. The teachers don't know this, but the gurlz are plotting. Heh! heh!

PESSIMIST

A pessimist always sees the down side. If an

Every silver lining has a cloud.

optimist says the cup is half full, the pessimist will say it's half empty (reverse, if liquid is deadly toxin). I am V. Worried that Worriers are essentially pessimists, as they are always thinking: 'What if?' ie: it is a perfectly nice day full of sunshine, cheer, little birdies humming in breeze Etck and everyone

will be skipping happily about in flimsy garb and
Worrier will say what if Hurricane Xerox emerges
from nowhere bringing Devastation in its wake?

LIFE-TIP: If you feel you have a tendency to look
on down-side, remember El Chubb's two fave
sayings:

'LIFE is just a bowl of Cherry stones' and
'When one door closes, another door closes.'

If you can do better than this, award yrself small
LIFE-enhancing treat – ie: a single Smartie Etck.

PETS

Are a V. Big solace in times of glume. Even a
goldfish is better than no pet, though watching
washing go round in machine is nearly as fun.

See CATS, DOGS, GERBILS, HORSES.

PHILOSOPHY

Philosophy is what you don't usually get to study
until 'A' level, which is a V. Big shame since it is
really the study of thought and how to think and
therefore one of the keys to the key to the key (if
there is one) to all of Yuman LIFE. It includes
seeking after wisdom generally in order to
understand the Nachur of the Yuniverse (at which
physics excels) and to werk out a moral philosophy

My Dream Pet (don't tell Rover)

(known as Ethics). Which is what we all need all the help we can get in doing.

'Philosophy' comes from Greek, and means 'a love of wisdom'. I Have a Dream, that one day I will have a clossal buke-lined study full of the Great Thoughts of V. Clever People, like they advertise in those brochures for encyclopaedias Etck, with everything in red leather with gold lettering Etck to make it look V. Old and Trustworthy. Then I wld travel with my BeLurved on a Great Philosophical Journey interrupted by bouts of Doing It and Making V. Brilliant Films, until I was the Wisest Person on Earth and people wld come to me for Guidance.

Philosophical Stuff includes Metaphysics (nachur and future of The Yuniverse), Idealism (whether the Werld is only Thought, and inside our heads), Materialism (whether the Werld is only Stuff – 'Matter' – outside our heads), Dualism (Thought and Stuff mixed together), Logic (how we werk things out), Ethics (Doing The Right Thing), Aesthetics (how we decide what's Byootiful Etck) and so on.

You can see from this brief Dirty Thumbnail sketch that Philosophy is a lot different to playing *DOLPHS*, *CITYSCAPE* Etck, and a pretty heavy business. Different countries also go in for different kinds of Philosophies, like the ones influenced by Buddhism in the East, by Materialism in Europe (Marxism Etck), by Science, by Art, and lately by

Komputer Science. A new Philosophy brought about by Komputers is called Chaos Theory, which sounds like the closest Philosophy has so far got to the LIFE of El Chubb and her Adored Family. If you want to get into Philosophy, you need to study it at skule if you can, and then at college or university, because it isn't something you can get together by reading half a buke and calling it a day.

PHOBIAS

Phobias are being scared of something for no good reason. At least, that's what the eggsperts say, but I'm scared of thingz quite a lot of the time and the reasons always seem perfectly good to me – it's reasonable to be scared my Adored Parents will have us all Repossessed frinstance, the way they stumble aimlessly through LIFE; reasonable to be scared I might wake up one morning to find myself turned into a giant pluke; reasonable to be scared God might not be Out There and the Werld is just a Virtual Reality game run by anoraked aliens from Ursa Minor Entertainments Corp.

Well, of course, it's not reasonable *reeeely*, because the odds on encountering these thingz statistically are about the size of my bra measurements. But there are zillions of types of Phobias, including fear of enclosed spaces (claustrophobia), open spaces (agoraphobia), water (hydrophobia), animals

Benjy has attack of Floor Phobia

(zoophobia) and floors (Benjyphobia), and it's a good idea to try to deal with them if you're afflicted by same, because otherwise it's like trying to run through LIFE as if it were a three-legged race, with this great mad, cackling, nagging, finger-wagging THING tied to your leg. And if they really get in the way of enjoying yrself, then you could need professional help like psychotherapy. DO see your doc if this is the case.

I have many minor obsessional habitz (fringe-twisting, touching things twice, fear of odd numbers Etck) but have just discovered brand-new one to add to long list of obsessional disorders Etck suffered by Chubb Family: Acrophobia. This is

A touch of Acrophobia on high kerb stones can make even short journeys problematic

related to Abseiling – an abnormal dread of heights. What is abnormal about this, for goodness' sake? I recall with horror becoming very dizzy crawling out onto a window-ledge to rescue an escaped Benjy when he was entrusted to the tender care of Yrs Truely, and had it not been for Said Sibling showing maturity beyond his years in turning around and V. Sweetly calming *moi* down until we could climb inside again, I don't know what would have happened. If we hadn't been on the ground floor I might have had a V. Serious Panic Attack.

Happy corner

PICNIC

One of El Chubb's favourite pastimes is going for
Picnics. *What?!* I hear you cry? You, who like best
to curl up with Rover, fudge, hot water bottle Etck?
Yes. *Moi*. I like to check out that Hurricane Xerox
is not lurking behind the sun, which means I will
watch the weather forecasts closely for many daze
before embarking on a Picnic adventure. But I like
it reminding me of my Yoof. I like packed lunches.
V. Crusty bread with loads of butter, cheese, jam,
strawberries, fudge Etck and a big flask of cherry
fizz. You then get to do absolutely nothing for four
hours except eat grub and gaze at little fluffy clouds,
dangle feet in tinkling stream, muse on wonders of
Mother Nachur Etck. Our local park, dog poo to the
left, rubbish dump to the right, is not the ideal
venue for this idyll – although I have been known to
sneak off here with Benjy and a couple of Teddies to
relive childhood. He likes to take a V. small packed
lunch for each Teddy, consisting of one Smartie, a
cherry tomato and a honey sandwich. A-ah BLESS.
But country-dwelling Teenage Worriers shld find
ample opps for this most cheap of pursuits.

PIERCING

Piercing noses, ears Etck used to be V. Naughty but
now most of Benjy's frendz' mums have rings

through their tongues Etck it is looking a bit old-fashioned to *moi*. Anyway, I don't even fancy pierced ears *moi*self, and am always looking for nice clip-on hoops to decorate my shell-like lobes (cross between those of Dumbo's relative and the Mad Hatter).

PIZZA

The fast food of the 80s is here to stay. Akshully, Pizzerias go back a lot futher than you might think: the first Pizzeria opened in America in 1895, and the boom in Pizza bars and restaurants really got going after WW2, when American servicemen returning from Italy created a demand for what was originally a Sicilian dish. However, it seems to me that in the age of Virtual Reality (see VIRTUAL REALITY) Etck the present method of Pizza deliveries on the back of mopeds driven by young escaped lunies with Visual Challenges is out of date and that it can only be a matter of time before a Fax-A-Pizza service is with us.

N.B. Lots of painting of Fruit Etck. But V. few Portraits of Pizza, I note.

PLAY

You may think, now you are a Teenage Worrier, that you are supposed to stop Playing. Most Adults, when they were about our age, thought the same thing, which is why they turned into the panic-stricken nervous wrecks who now rool our lives. But the secret is to go on Playing for the rest of yr LIFE. How to play

    a) Cheaply and
    b) Legally

is the main prob, as Adventure Playgrounds Etck are beginning to lose their appeal (although a simple swing still feels grate to El Chubb – am I retarded? Worry, worry).

It is no coincidence that musicians *Play* music, or that actors put on *Plays*, or that professional sport people *Play* sport . . . Playing is about having a good time and if you can find werk that is fun, then you will never have to stop Playing for the rest of your LIFE. You can see who really enjoys their werk in the Adult Werld – musicians, obsessive scientists, inventors, footballers, actors Etck.

L. Chubb's LIFE-TIP: Have FUN.

POCKET MONEY

This is like wages-for-kids. It should be yours to spend exactly as you like and it shouldn't be stopped, really, 'cos you can't get sacked by your parents and the only way their wages are stopped is if they get fired. But . . . whatever your foks give you, big or small, it is never enough. It is, though,

probably all they can afford (unless they are V.V.
Rich – and if they are, then they aren't being mean,
just trying to let you discover meaning of money
Etck Etck, blah drone). Teenagers, like pensioners,
come in all shapes, sizes, colours and characters. But
what they have in common is that they are Poor.

See also, JOBS, MONEY.

POETRY

One of LIFE's great solaces, Poetry can comfort
Teenage Worriers in times of glume and dume and
it is V. Imp to write a lot of it at our age. In fact, if
you have got to 17 without writing a poem, it may
be worth sitting down and having a go.

An essential LIFE-Item in El Chubb's artillery for
fending off dume is a personal Limerick. It can be
done even if you have V. Difficult name like my
own. Viz:

> *There was a young woman called Scarlett*
> *Who objected to rhyming with harlot*
> *'Don't call me a whore,'*
> *She declared with a roar*
> *'Or I'll soon give you something to snarl at.'*

NB This will work equally well with Charlotte. If
you are called Betty you can nick my other one:

There was a young person named Letty
Who said of a bloke she had met, 'He
Would be perfectly nice
If ploughing through ice
For he puts me in mind of a Yeti.'

I'm qu. proud of the double rhyme in the second line and am wondering if a career as a lyricist beckons (phew, blush). I had been working on one for Adam but was having trouble ('Macadam'? 'Madam'? Etck). And what about Daniel? ('Spaniel'?). Answers on a postcard please.

POLITICS

Harry Stotle (not really! *Aristotle*, you lunes), the famous Greek thinker and Person, said that 'Man is a Political Animal', and I think he must have meant Gurlz too. What was he on about? The dictionary says Politics is about governing, and when we were all stumbling around in woad clubbing each other Etck, there prob wasn't a lot of governing going on, but maybe that's why Harry Stotle thought the Idea caught on in the first place. As Yuman Groups got larger, they had to werk out how to organize themselves, agree on Leaders, establish Laws Etck, so they didn't have to go round clubbing each other at random all the time but could work out who were the Right People to Club and who weren't, which

is pretty much how Politics werks today.

Most Teenage Worriers are V. Political, which means they hate politicians but care V. Much about the things that politicians ought to be caring about. It is Teenage Worriers who do V. Brave actions like tunnelling under motorways to try to Save Trees Etck. We know that writing to MPs will never achieve so much as Direct Action and we also know

A little pun – Polly tics

that MPs who complain about their salaries Etck are Out-of-Touch with most folk who are

a) Earning less
b) Earning nothing.

But in my better moments I can't help thinking that Politics would be a V. Good Thing to go into if you think you're a strong enough person to keep Yr Principles against all the pressures you come up against. If this is yr LIFE-choice, Good Luck.

NB Campaign for the new Teenage Worriers' Party (see PARTIES ho ho).

PROMISCUITY

Means sleeping around, which has always been V. Acceptable for Boyz but not for Gurlz. AIDS has given everyone a new reason not to do this (although there are still V. few Teenage Worriers who are as concerned about AIDS as I think they shld be), but my main reason wld be that I only Fancy V. few people and the chances of them fancying me back are pretty slight so how wld I get the chance to be Promiscuous? I wouldn't want to be Promiscuous with someone I didn't fancy, but maybe that's what Promiscuous people do – just bonk away with anything bonkable, to get practice. Hmmmmm. It wld be V. tiring.

PROSTITUTION

It is hard to see why Prostitutes are so frowned on for selling their bods since Boxers and Page Three Gurlz get a high price for what they look like and are Popular Heroes, Heroines, opening fêtes, motor shows Etck. There is always the possibility that you might meet Famous Movie Star Huge Rant, or the Minister of State for Naughty Bits in yr werk, but since this is a family buke, I feel I should point out that although you can certainly buy SEX, you can't buy Lurve. And since SEX and Lurve are V. closely acquainted, paying for it seems a bit misguided to *moi*, though many Boyz (and some Gurlz) look at it differently and say that SEX and Lurve are not the same. Hrrmph.

Sadly, brothels, seedy rooms in Kings X Etck are V. Likely places in which to get an STD (Sexually Transmitted Disease), of which AIDS is one. Also, the Prostitutes are usually at the mercy of vile pimps who start out being nice, giving them roof over head Etck but end up taking most of their earnings and beating them up, so it doesn't look like a V. Good way of earning dosh to *moi*.

It is V. Sad to think of Teenage Worriers, who should be at Dawn of LIFE Etck, ending up doing things they don't enjoy to panting politicians, travelling salesmen Etck because they didn't get any GCSEs, or if they did, they didn't get a job. Even so, most Teen Worriers would rather beg in streets than exchange their vital juices with people they don't fancy. And I am certainly of the latter persuasion.

PSYCHIATRIST

I am also including Therapists here, because they all try to help you when you think your head's going to explode. Most of them look at you with a weird kind of Listening Face. Benjy has a Teddy that looks like this, with its head on one side and an expression like someone trying to smile with a tummy-ache. The Analyst may have studied Clement – sorry, Sigmund – Freud (all problems about whether or not you have a Willy), Carl Jung (all problems about the Collective Unconscious, eg: the clientele

Wld this be my fate if I slouched to the couch?
And if so, could I tell?

of the Dog and Duck on Saturdays) or Melanie Klein
(all problems about recognizing a Breast is part of a
Whole Person – this is supposed to be just an Infant
Phase, but most Boyz I know haven't realized this).

It may be better to talk to yr Best Frend than go
to Analysts if you have V. Bad Lurve probs, because
it is V. Hard to get therapy on the NHS anyway,
although the NHS ones are at least trained and some
of them are V. Good if you are desperately Unhappy.

Actually, I wld really like to go myself, about
having to say 'banana' instead of that word about
dying that rhymes with 'breath' as I feel it is in
danger of becoming more of a phobia than an
eccentricity. Turning lights on and off twice and
bending down to touch the floor again when I drop
something are also beginning to be anoying habits
. . . but would an Analyst just start blaming my
Only Mother and Wrecking our Relationship, I
wonder?

I suppose I'd better wait till I am really
desperate – otherwise, what will there be to turn to?

I must muse on these and other things while
considering whether Agony Aunts, about whom I
was less than kind in my first humble volume, are in
fact a cheaper option than Analysts or Therapists.
Pouring out your probs is half the battle, they say,
in this Cruel Werld. Sometimes, just keeping a
diary to pour your heart out into might be enough
. . . but if you are V. depressed, or have a frend who
is, DO go and get advice.

See also DEPRESSION, PHOBIAS.

CHAPTER TEN
QQQQQQze and RRRRRRze

Dearest Reader,

You will not be surprised to find that Daniel did not come at the appointed hour. Nor at the hour after that. Nor the hour after that either. Arg. Perhaps he saw Adam running down the steps after me – and thought we were still together!

Home, distraught, to find Father in tears, clasping scrunched-up piece of paper in one hand and a half empty bottle of whisky in the other.

Glume! It must be a terrible review of his buke!

But no.

It was worse.

He had found a note on the table:

> *Alice.*
> *I'll pick you up at ten.*
> *Neville.*

'She'sh left me. Left USH. Packed her bagsh and flown the nesht. Never to bid goodbye! Left thish note.'

And my Adored Only Father, about whom I have not always been kind, collapsed in a torrent of grief.

'There'sh only one way out,' he wept.

I phoned the Samaritans in a panic and they tried to

talk to him but he is too tearful to speak, and in any case
had been referring to the other half of the bottle of whisky.
I sit with him all night, sleeping only fitfully, constantly
awoken by thoughts of my Dear Father, as occasioned by
his regular noisy visits to the loo, caused by the effects of
the bottle of whisky and jamming DIY lock on the door.
How could my Mother leave us all? Her Only Benjy, too?
Without even explaining? And for some seedy millionaire?
How callous! How materialistic!

  How . . . um . . . predictable.

255

I have ignored my Only Family and forsaken them in pursuit of boyz who Don't Care! I should have seen this coming and talked to my Mother before it got out of hand . . .

Granny Chubb comes to rescue first thing in morning. I do not tell her whole truth as Father begs me not to. I beg HIM not to End It All. He looks somewhat surprised, having been cheered up by his Only Mother making him a cup of tea the texture of treacle and a hot water bottle complete with a little stripy, hand-knitted cover of trains and teddies that she'd kept since he was 7 . . .

Meanwhile, I am on the phone to the Komputer Empire founded by Neville. He has been in Barbados for last 6 months, lies secretary.

'But he's stolen my Mother!' I scream.

The secretary becomes somewhat huffy at this point, declaring the seedy Neville's loyalty to his large family of two ex-wives and one current one, thus confirming my worst fears of his adulterous behaviour.

Ring police to say Only Mother has been kidnapped, but they are deeply uninterested when I let slip about the note.

'Sorry, love, but this sounds like a domestic incident. Your Mother clearly went willingly.'

We will have to get a detective agency to track down the dastardly Neville.

I trail glumly to skule two hours late to find Spiggy back. False alarm re dying grandad (evidently grandads are hardier than aunts), who has perked up a treat. She tells me Daniel proposed last night. I consider showing her his letter to moi, but feel I cannot stoop so low, even with

my shoulders. Clearly, he thought I wld do while she was
away, but when he heard she was back, he didn't even
bother coming to meet me. I do not care any more, only
thing that matters is return of Mother, happiness of Father
Etck.

Just as I am pondering these Deep and Meaningful
events, the skule secretary tells me that a note marked
URGENT: ATTENTION L. CHUBB has arrived.

Panic.

My Father! My Mother! Banana! Mayhem! Murder!
Tragedy! Betrayal! Spokeshave! Etck.

Trembling, I open it.

Dear Scarlett,

My aunt is very well, thank you. Candice, as far as I
know, is in Los Angeles, not that I care. Whoever gave you
the idea that I did, was gravely mistaken. I am, however,
interested in seeing you if you are interested in seeing me.

I shall wait for you outside the school gates tomorrow
morning at eight o'clock. This will give you a chance to
think things over. I have no desire to force unwanted
attentions on you, but I was under the impression (silly me,
perhaps) that we were on the verge of something rather
special.

Yours,
Adam.

What an amazing note. So sensitive. So caring. So
UNlike Daniel Hope's puke-making, yeechy, grovelling,
Frills & Swoon type phrases.

How foolish I had been . . . How could I risk the affections of one so serious, honest and true for a fickle fule like Daniel Hopeless?

Another ghastly night beckons with its scaly, rabid claws of Insomnia . . . comforting Father and Benjy while waiting to hear from appalling Only Mother. Pretend to Benjy she had to go away for a couple of nights. If only it were true. How could she do it?????! How will we ever find her??

Father, however, in somewhat better spirits as Granny Chubb now cosily installed and making us all boiled eggs with soldiers – including Father, who says he has not had same since he was boy.

Search Yellow Pages for Private Detective Agencies in vain. Sit weeping by phone. Surely Only Mother will ring . . .

QUALIFICATIONS

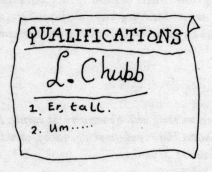

What you need to fulfil LIFE's missions. Once you have chosen yr career, you need to check out, blah drone.

See also CAREER, EXAMS, JOBS.

QUARK

What Quarks MIGHT look like magnified 200,000 zillion times. If they weren't hypothetical...

I always mix up the diff kinds of Quarks, and end up concluding that fundamental units of matter that make up LIFE, the Yuniverse and Everything akshully consist of cream cheese. This is, however, a different meaning of Quark, and one that maybe doesn't matter so much to a guide to LIFE, though I'm sure those people who don't mind eating meals that smell like old socks, recently occupied loos Etck wld disagree.

Quarks are 'subatomic particles', ie: to whit: V. Small Bitz that make all the Stuff in the World hold together. Quarks show how Difficult it has got to be a Scientist these days, and maybe why some Scientists are going back to Religion for explanations for Thingz. Because you can't *see* them, even with V. Powerful microscopes, clever instruments Etck. They're *hypothetical*, ie: worked out by sums Etck. The physicist who figured them out said he chose the title from a werd the writer James Joyce used in his V. Baffling little buke *Finnegans Wake*, something I have *moi*self attempted to read and which I wld have thought cld have been written by Benjy, but I am prepared to believe Cleverer Persons than El Chubb, viz Ashley and even (sometimes) Adored Mother, who says I will appreciate it in time.

RAINY DAY

While away more Rainy Daze by finding writers whose names are anagrams of food: Keats and steak? Proust and sprout? Yeats and yeast?) Build an Ark — why not? Especially if it is VERY rainy.

Many happy hours can be whiled away compiling and weeping over these: photos, letters, scrapbooks. Granny Chubb has V. Good albums, a page of which I have reproduced below. In fact, I think I shld consider publishing them in their entirety and

Me & Ron. Clacton.

Dandelion 1954

Dear Mr Chubb,
You're fired
Yours
F. Atcat

Letter from Ron's boss.

My first teabag.

make fortune Etck. That old *Country Diary of an Edwardian Lady* did V. Well, although it is less sure that the *Urban Jottings of an Elizabethan Charlady* has quite the same ring.

See also SENTIMENTAL JOURNEY.

RAVES

Divides Teenage Worriers, because Gurlz usually start dancing younger and do it better than Boyz, though much dancing at Raves Etck does not require fancy footwork but demented flailing about as if with massive electric charge up Beumb. This kind of dancing suits El Chubb because requiring Zilch Expertise, but if you're going to do it you're supposed to do it for a long time without getting tired, which is not easy.

See also DANCE.

REBELS

These are the Yoof you read about. The ones who stay out late, sniffing glue, snorting coke, having orgies Etck Etck. You spend a lot of time thinking: 'When will my mother let me do that?' This means you are not a rebel.

RECYCLING

See ENVIRONMENT.

RELIGION

Sometimes when I see Benjy in hysterics about the floor I think that if he believed in a God who was a cross between Father Christmas and Batman he would Know No Fear. I have V. Mixed Feelings about godz, and though I think I prob believe in some kind of Superior Being I am not sure that the

Many Teenage Worriers still have an image of God like above...

Benjy's version...

one Granny Chubb believes in is quite the one for me, though He/She/It seems to have made her very Contented.

263

Maybe it's the Christian one being called 'God the Father' Etck that causes the prob, because that makes me think of my Adored Father, and much as I care about him, imagining God like that makes me think of a Big Bearded Man with the Angel Gabriel on his right hand and a can of lager in his left, arguing in V. Deep Old Testament Charlton Heston-type voices about the access code for *CITYSCAPE*.

I think I will need a diff kind of God, or a diff kind of religion – possibly like the Buddhist one, which is Somewhat Worryingly based on the inevitability of Yuman suffering, glume, despond Etck. Buddha (it means 'enlightened one') taught that whatever you Desire is changing all the time and so are you, so Desiring things is bound to make you Unhappy. You have to search, therefore, for something beyond the comings and goings of Yuman LIFE, ie, to whit, viz: Enlightenment.

El Chubb's two-watt brain has concluded that the Buddha thought LIFE isn't something fixed like *being*, but a moving stream of *becoming*. Nothing is for ever, so wanting masses of dosh, power over people, facelifts, fame Etck are meaningless. The only thing worth becoming is Truely Enlightened, which is, I suppose, like being in Heaven. I'm not sure I could cope yet with all the sacrifices this Way of LIFE seems to involve (though if you take it seriously enough I suppose they don't seem like sacrifices), and the position of Buddhist teaching on

Fudge is V. Difficult to establish, but it's a V. Interesting antidote to all materialism, interfering with Nachur Etck.

Islam is a huge and V. Influential religion in certain parts of the Arab, African and Eastern Werld. Along with Judaism and Christianity, it is a 'monotheistic' religion, ie: one all-powerful God. It started in the Arab werld in the 7th Century, and in Arabic Islam means 'surrender'. Allah, the Islamic God, is all-powerful for Muslims, so the idea is to surrender to Allah's will. If you are a Muslim, you will have to face Mecca and pray 5 times a day, fast on the 9th month of the Muslim year (Ramadan), avoid alcohol, gambling and lending money for profit (usury). Praying 5 times a day is no prob for a Teenage Worrier such as *moi*; I think Adored Father wld definitely benefit from Muslim teachings on alcohol and gambling; and lending money for profit is certainly no prob for Ali El Chubb since I never have any; but some forms of Islam do not have a great record on their attitude to us Gurlz, which I have to say puts *moi* off – although I have to admit that none of the other religions have been much better in the past.

In general, I don't much care for bossy godz who demand big personal sacrifices from people too young, poor or confused to know better. But some kind of god in yr LIFE can be good for Worriers, and some people with V. Strong Beliefs do seem to Worry less, even about V. Big Worries like Banana.

REWARDS

MAJOR LIFE-TIP: Reward yrself at every opportunity. You got dressed? You went to skule? You spent whole hour without whingeing? You deserve a reward! Choose from LIFE's rich tapestry of fun: fudge (nosh of all kinds), bubble baths, a bunch of flowers, tapes, bukes, frendz' nights out . . . whatever.

ROMEO

V. Good name for famed Teenage Lurver. Naturally, because written by an Adult (although admittedly the V. talented, and not, as far as we know, gay, W. Spokeshave) Young Lurve goes badly wrong and we are all supposed to learn a lesson about burying our differences (which is better than burying our Teenagers).

ROOMS

The Teenage Worrier's Ideal bedroom is Kool: spacious, uncluttered, tastefully equipped with hi-tech modems that zap you into the Internet and with no hint of a younger or older sibling, or indeed your younger self. You will have seen this room in a magazine. There are no visible clothes, because they have all been packed away into a hi-tech super storage unit from *Adobe Style* (£490). The sound system will be minuscule in size but gigantic decibel-wise (*Adobe Sounds* £596.99). The walls will be snow-white (*Adobe Tints* £7.50 a can) with a section reserved for graffiti which will include the signatures of all your mates plus witty and pithy comments by yourself about the Nachur of the Yuniverse, best band, Etck. The elegant futon-style bed (*Adobe Furnishings* £306) is covered in a sumptuous yet understated duvet (*Adobe Fabrics*

267

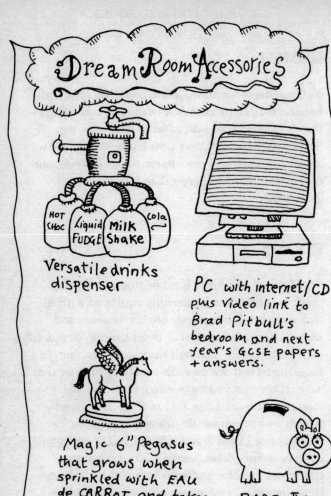

Dream Room Accessories

Versatile drinks dispenser

HOT CHOC | Liquid FUDGE | Milk Shake | Cola

PC with internet/CD plus video link to Brad Pitbull's bedroom and next year's GCSE papers + answers.

Magic 6" Pegasus that grows when sprinkled with EAU de CARROT and takes me flying at Midnight. (Eat your heart out, Sigmund Freud).

BABE: The magic Piggy-bank that's always full of tenners.

Automatic sock-sorter

Fold-away FACE ➔ with night-time Acne
-banish mode

water bed
with sea horses

Arg. Have just discovered this
is unsound as seahorses are
threatened species. Benjy has
suggested jelly fish.

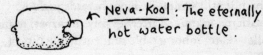

Neva-Kool : The eternally
hot water bottle.

£37.60). The huge, Manhattan loft-style windows
will be covered by venetian blinds (*Adobe Glasshouse*
£245.99). The lighting, operated by dimmer
switches, (*Adobe Illuminations* £209.76) will
individually gleam on those items which express the
Individual You. They include: silk screen print by
classy photographer of urban wastescape *(Adobe
Printshop* £78.90 including clip frame), bonsai tree
(*Adobe Orientale* £36) and a designer soft toy of vast
but charmless dimensions (*Adobe Care* £39.99) to
show you have soft heart.

You've clocked this room in the mag.

If you're smart, you will also have clocked the
two-page advertisement for *ADOBE* – FOR THOSE
WHO WANT TO TURN THEIR HABITAT
INTO A＊NEST, which runs a few pages after the
'objective' feature on the Teenage Room.

＊ and if this is a nest, I'm an aardvark.

The Teenage Worrier's Real Room is like this:

Marginally larger than the bed in the *Adobe Room*
above. It has sky-blue walls with nursery rhyme
freeze. Bunk beds – one of which is prob still
occupied by 10-year-old sibling. Dark-brown pre-
war clothes cupboard that you used to knock on the
back of hoping Aslan would leap out and whisk you
off to Narnia. The doors do not close and it is
overflowing with stuff, only a small proportion of
which is still wearable. Floor hazards include:
plasticine ingrained irretrievably in carpet; rogue
roller-skate; innumerable unidentifiable bits of

plastic and fluff; socks without partners; pens and pen tops ditto; gerbil poo; myriad UFOs (unidentified fallen objects). Yr attempts to cover nursery rhyme frieze with posters are charming but without obvious merit either in terms of artistic or interllekshual content – in addition to which, they are crooked. There is a bare light bulb hanging from the centre of the ceiling as you couldn't stand the Winnie-the-Pooh lampshade any more and ripped it out in a frenzy. Yr parents could not or would not afford a replacement. Yr duvet cover is off-white as you have turned it pattern-side down (the pattern being dinosaurs). The curtains are lurid and flowery, having come from some old aunt's lair (yr parents never bothered to buy pretty ones for your room even when you were a baba) but since window is tiny at least there isn't much curtain on view. Sadly, they do have frilly pelmet. Yr attempts to dismantle this only resulted in frayed pelmet.

The only bit of yr room comparable with the *Adobe* one is graffiti corner, where your sibling has drawn a lot of pictures and rude words like 'poo-bum' and 'fart-willy' in indelible marker. The small corner of this midden you can call yr own is shelf above yr bunk bed. On it are: mugs encrusted with green fur; pony books; horror books that you hide the covers of as you don't want to wake up in middle of night with ghouls looking at you (also because they have 'banana' werds in titles); ancient eyeless teddy, ditto elephant, ditto monkey, ditto pink blob; wobbly pile of comics; stack of oddments.

Oddments gather in most corners of most houses except those of pathologically tidy. They include: paperclips, drawing pins, conkers, fluff, dried-up brushes, bits of sellotape, stickers, batteries, tiny bits of felt, dried-up chewing gum, mysterious keys, tissues, thread, buttons, teaspoons, V. Small bottles . . . (*make yr own list here . . .*)

You compare yr lack of room with the style magazine's surfeit of room. And you . . . prefer yr own.

It's cosy. If only it were tidy . . .

TIDYING TIP:

Do it tomorrow.

When tomorrow comes, put everything except duvet and pillow under your bed.

Fish out as necessary.

NB If you can be bothered, put duvet and pillow on yr bed.

ADOBE room.   MY room.
Spot the difference. N.B. pictures drawn at night time.

CHAPTER ELEVEN
SSSSSSSSes

Decide to attempt to drown own sorrows by looking at my film noire of Urban Glume . . . Ghastly whining sounds from camera convince me I have overrun film already, but after usual cursing and cranking of wrong buttons, levers Etck am able to replay what the camera has 'seen' from my window. Glume deepens at realization that one fixed camera filming for two mins each day is V.V. Unsatisfactory way of capturing cutting-edge dekay:

First two mins: *Pavement.*

Second two mins: *Boy (NOT sufficiently urchin-like, alas, as well washed and akshully in skule uniform!!!!) playing hopscotch.*

Third two mins: *Rather nice-looking dog (on lead! Grr!) NOT doing a poo. Followed by postman wheeling bike and WHISTLING. (How could he DO that in face of wicked Govt's decimation of his future Etck.) Sudden fear he may be postman Aggy's mother ran off with, assuaged by realization they are abroad . . .*

Fourth two mins: *Plump gurgling baby in buggy pushed by cheerful-looking parents (TWO of them! One male! One female!); more pavement; a girl in a flowery frock skipping, with an* ice cream cone.

ARGH! What has happened to my VISIONE?

ARGH. What has happened to my Visione?

My street looks like some perfect place from the 1950s . . . dogs on leads, jolly whistling postmen, hopscotch, skipping, married couples with babies!! Am just about to tear up film in despair (while secretly wondering whether LIFE really does go on as Normally as this and I only see the Worst Side because I am a Teenage Worrier . . .) when my heart leaps up at the sight of the

Fifth two mins: A cruising car containing a seedy-looking punter and yes! A hooker! The door . . . opens . . . the woman gets in . . . Street life at last!

But wait.

I am frozen in horror.

I recognize those red high heels.

My Mother.

Dear Reader,
Do not faint (though I nearly did). My Mother has not (I hope) gone on the streets to sell her body. She is obviously getting into Neville's car! I have video evidence! We will be able to trace the car and save her from a Fate worse than Banana . . .

Father and Granny Chubb are dipping their soldiers into boiled eggs and leafing lovingly through snaps of Dad on a Donkey aged 5 as I hurtle in waving the camera about wildly. Using Granny Chubb's powerful magnifying device we decipher number plate of the Neville-Mobile, and Father, replete with nursery food, rather relaxedly dials the cops. I stop him, saying they will not follow up a woman going off with her fancy man, they have enough to do with chasing yobs in joy-riding escapades pretending they are Beverly Hills style cops Etck or comforting little old ladies with dachshunds stuck under their baths . . .

But Only Father is smarter than I thought. He pretends Mother has been abducted. He got number of car. Urgent they trace it Etck. It seems to werk. They will get onto it straight away, they say. Should have news of Mother V. Soon. I thought I heard my Father murmur 'No rush' but I must have been mistaken.

Benjy to bed with Granny Chubb, so sleep a little better, accompanied by fragment of Hope . . .

Perhaps all will be well . . . my Mother home and, though I struggle to suppress the selfish gene, my bosom (well, sort of) swells (prinks?) at prospect of reunion with Adam . . .

School *more computers NOW!*

A lot of rubbish is talked about Skules in the opinion of *moi*, particularly nowadaze when Govts are concluding that they don't akshully know why half the things in the World happen, despite all the posh edukashons of Ministers, Civil Servants Etck, and now they're trying to make out that if it wasn't for luny teachers in denims letting children run around in woad Etck, it wldn't have got like this.

Skules are many different things, because there are many different kinds of pupils, viz: you and *moi* for a start. If you wanted to be V. Meen about Skules, you might just say they were places to keep children out of the way of their parents, so Govts built jails for Yoof called Skules and tortured them with Lessons. It is prob true to say that most of what children learn about Reading, Writing and Maths before they become Teenage Worriers cld be taught to them V. Intensively in about a year and the rest of the time they cld spend playing conkers, Doctors and Nurses, hiding in skips Etck.

But we all know that loads of Skule is V. Boring, so I've tried V. Hard to think of some positive, LIFE-affirming bits about Skule, and I *think* I've succeeded.

Although Skules are partly just ways of solving the prob of where to put children now they can't be sent up chimneys any more Etck, good teachers can be an inspiration, espesh if they believe in making

276

That teacher's REALLY tough

Yeh. He asked me to tell him my date of birth. From MEMORY!

you think hard about thingz you don't normally think about, instead of packing you full of unrelated facts you don't understand. For children living in V. Rough housing, a good Skule can be the most welcoming place they go to, or it wld be if Govts didn't keep encouraging people in nice housing to send their nice children somewhere else, and let the Skules in rough districts get worse. For that matter, a good local Skule can also be the best way to show V. Privileged Children about Ways of LIFE quite diff to theirs. Frinstance, at Hazel's posh Gurlz' Academy they all get given Porsches Etck on their 17th birthday, but it doesn't stop them from putting slugs in her tennis shoes 'cos she's Gay. And at Daniel Hope's Skule they think a high-rise is something their pater (Latin for Dad) gives the chauffeur, but the bullying goes on even werse than at Sluggs. Also, there are loads of Druggies at posh Skules 'cos they have lots more money to chuck around.

277

I wldn't say Slugg's Comp is likely to turn out an above-average number of Nobel Prizewinners or anything, but it is a meeting place for me and all my frendz in a place that doesn't cost us money just to sit down and it *does* make Clever Kids cleverer without becoming Obnoxious and Not-So-Clever Kids feel they amount to something. It also has a lot of pretty interesting thingz you can do in lessons and out, and it mixes a lot of different kinds of people. Just the same, I'd rather be out of it and getting on with becoming Werld Famous film-maker Etck. And if Mr Hesseltine (our head teacher) is reading this, I'm sure he'll hasten my departure V. Kwick.

See also EXAMS.

SCUFFING DMS ON PAVEMENT

Major LIFE experience of TWs available at a street corner near you. Campaign for 'Scuffing Cheap trainers on Pavement' division of this group, as it's not what you scuff but the way that you scuff it what counts.

SENTIMENTAL JOURNEY

This is L. Chubb's Romantick way of having a clear-out. You can quite easily spend the whole holidays doing this if you take enough time crying over each item.

But do you REALLY want to hang on to your first Incy-wincey Pony and its bride's bridle? Or books like *Miss Mouse's Marmalade Adventure*, *Telling the Time with Mr Worm*, *Ant, Bucket, Crash!*, or *Purple Penguin's Book of Shades*? (Of course you do: I got enthralled by how Miss Mouse extricated all her little mouselets from the gooey marmalade jar, narrowly escaping clutches of evil cat Etck.)

Other V. Moving items include V. Early drawings that look like bits of wire wool surrounded by nits and say: 'Hapy mOutH's Dai' or 'I LuV yo baddy', but it is upsetting to find them crumpled up under your bed instead of lovingly pressed between the scented pages of your Mother's scrapbook.

And what is this? A birthday card from your first

Lurve, who was a curly-haired bruiser of 7 and invited you to his party, where you got over-excited and were sick in his mother's laundry basket . . .

Your intention to create a whole bag full of rubbish is undermined by the affection you feel for the past. A good compromise is to chuck a few of your sibling's favourite toys out instead. This will create the extra room you need at no personal expense. Draw the line at the Teddy he/she actually goes to bed with, if you want to escape with yr LIFE.

SERVANTS

Domestic servants are making a V. Big come-back! Surprise surprise . . . As the 'work-rich-time-poor' people find they have more dosh but less time, so they are employing the 'work-poor-but-time-rich' fok to do their cleaning, baby-sitting, even shopping Etck. Granny Chubb earned her living like this until V. Recently and there is nowt wrong with it except that the gap between Rich and Poor, instead of getting smaller as you wld hope in Civilized Werld, is actually growing. But, as usual, I have a democratic solution . . .

I have personally always fantasized about having a butler ever since falling in love with Batman's butler Alfred while watching *Batman Forever* with Benjy. Benjy was much too young for it and dreamt

Naturally, one would prefer not to use the same kitchen as one's cook. But times are hard.

that the floor was full of drain-covers made of dirty grey blancmange through which he wld plunge into Penguin's Lair at every step. But can you imagine the joys of lying on yr hammock calling for a couple of strawberry milk shakes and yr Ferrari to be

281

delivered and finding that a slender cove (dressed as a penguin, as it happens) shimmers up to you to grant yr every whim?

Naturally in El Chubb's Equal Society, everyone wld have butlers, even the butlers. *How wld this be?* I hear you cry. First, everyone gets a turn at *being* a butler – say for three months. Then they get a butler of their own. Then, after their turn is up, if they want another butler they have to *be* a butler again and so on . . . Luxury and penury for all!

SEX/SEX EDUCATION

El Chubb has, of course, dealt with this V. Fascinating subject many times in earlier tomes, but since Teenage Worriers, along with everyone else, never tire of reading about it, I make no excuses for including it again; in fact I'd probably have to have a good excuse if I didn't.

I also have to face the fact that my views on SEX are to some extent guesswork at the moment, though I have high hopes of Adam, of course. It is V. Diff to be a Teenage Worrier who has not Done It because any magazine Worried about its circulation now puts 'The SEX Issue' on its cover, tabloid newspapers put SEX stories on the front page and the opening skirmishes of World War Three somewhere in the Sports section, and generally you feel that if you haven't Done It yet it's

like standing on the street by yourself outside a party that everybody else seems to have gone to.

El Chubb arms herself against this particular Worry with the following:

1) SEX is something people lie about more often than almost anything else (except maybe Dosh), and espesh Boyz for whom SEX is a big part of their egos. Gurlz sometimes make their SEX lives up to make you jealous, or stop you realizing they're just as confused about it as you are, and Boyz sometimes make it up to show you (and each other) what a Big Deal they are, and how much you'd regret it if you missed their Once In A LIFEtime offer.

2) At the moment SEX is against the law in Britain if you're under 16. This does not mean a large policeman disguised as Rover will spring out from under yr bed and arrest you for nibbling yr BeLurved's ear, frinstance, but if you are caught nibbling V. Intimate partz you and your partner cld be in for some V. Embarrassing questions from Adults.

3) Even without Worrying about AIDS, SEX itself is a risky part of LIFE, because it involves V. Strong (and sometimes Uncontrollable, phew) Emotions.

Personally, I wld hate a big Promising, Wonderful thing like SEX to ever be a Habit, and the Risky bit of it seems V. Exciting. However, I am not sure I know enough about *moi*self to be ready for qu. that much Excitement yet, but with the Right Person I feel sure that I cld trust another Yuman Bean with my emotions.

4) I do not want to get Pregnant, or catch an STD (Sexually Transmitted Disease) if I Do It with someone I don't know just for the sake of Doing It.

Having said all that, and having read what various Clever People have to say about how complicated SEX is, you don't have to be a Genius to realize that Nachur has got on with it pretty well for zillions of years, and so have Yuman Beans or else we wouldn't all be here and (mostly) still sane. It is now a regular part of skule LIFE, however, to go in for something called SEX EDUKASHUN. Skules have been told by the Govt that they should emphasize Family Values, Traditional Morality Etck, when they tell Teenage Worriers about SEX, though many skules prefer to treat it as a Health Ishoo (showing Teenage Worriers trembling on brink of SEXuality how to look after their Bods Etck). Since many members (and I used the word advisedly) of the House of Horrors clearly have V. Big Probs re Traditional Morality, viz: Sleaze, Bitz on the Side, Money for Questions Etck, I'm not sure they are the right people to be offering this advice, however.

NB V. Good contraceptive leaflets are available at your doc's. Read thoroughly.

See also PROMISCUITY.

SHOPPING

Teenage Worriers do a lot of this, mainly for clothes and mainly window-shopping due to lack of dosh. Rebels (see REBELS above) do shop-lifting but L. Chubb does not recommend due to

a) Terror
b) Guilt.

Shopping for presents is the one kind you *have* to do at least once a year. If you have a family it gets to be about four times a year. Add frendz' birthdays and that's all your money gone without ever getting a thing for yourself. Adults wld not put up with this. **CAMPAIGN FOR TEENAGE WORRIERS' SHOPPING ALLOWANCE.** Boyz have an easy time with prezzies as they can get away with a mouldy old bunch of flowers or a cheapo box of chocs and everyone will think they are V. Nice, Trustworthy Etck for bothering at all. Gurlz have to spend hours thinking about what people would actually LIKE. Maybe we shld all just stick to fudge 'n' flowers. V. Easy.

PRESENT-SHOPPING TIPS:
(Have revised these in accordance with new Insight above)
Parents: Fudge
Siblings: Fudge
Frendz: Fudge
Aunts Etck: Flowers.
(NB Can substitute chocs Etck for fudge if you prefer, as you will note that edibles are given to those you see most of and therefore can be consumed by yourself.)

SIGHTSEEING

V. Good way to find out about LIFE's rich tapestry is to delve into the Past. It is poss to see quite a lot of monuments, sights Etck for free, espesh if you are a good walker and live in London. Skules are sometimes V. Good at organizing trips to places like this, and you should encourage yr teachers to consider it. Remember they need to be told it's for improvement of Yr Mind Etck, rather than opportunity to get off lessons, fiddle about with Darren or Sharon in the back seat of coach Etck.

SKIN

Normal Teenage Worrier's Skin →

zit → ᴑ ← oily patch

o⊦ ← pluke

☰ ← Dry patch

Skin is V. Extraordinary Stuff. It is, of course, just as well we have it, or we wld all have to go round as Skellingtons, which wld not be anything like as nice as the arrangements we have now, though praps if we were all like that it wouldn't matter.

Teenage Worriers do a lot of their Worrying about Skin, espesh whether it's too greasy, too spotty Etck Etck. There are zillions of Skin preparations we spend our meagre quantities of loot on, in the hope they will make us look more like Supermodels, Hollywood stars or Hazel (gnash). But the cheapest and best methods we cld find for looking after our Skin just come down to eating fruit, drinking water, avoiding chocs (shame and not definite evidence about any of this anyway, grrrr), not smoking, and not spending so much of our lives indoors in centrally heated skules, homes, glumey klubs Etck that our Skin never finds out what fresh

287

air akshully is. This is the sort of Good Advice that Teenage Worriers, including *moi*, find pretty hard to follow, and that's V. Good News for the cosmetics business, which gets people to part with vast fortunes for thingz they cld take care of themselves.

The colour of people's Skins has caused a lot of trouble, and when you come to consider that the reason someone is black, white, olive-coloured or whatever is just to do with how much of this pigment or that is in the epidermis, or outer layer, it doesn't seem like a big enough difference to account for all the fuss there's been over it. Pigments are there as sunscreens, and the only reason for the different-coloured pigments is what kind of exposure to the sun y're likely to get, which is why people from hot countries are darker. And that's *all*.

Underneath that is the dermis, which is packed with all kinds of interesting Stuff (except that if you can *see* how interesting it all is, you prob need to get to a hospital fast), including blood vessels, muscles, nerves, sweat glands and the little tubes that keep yr hair on. If the nerves in Yr Skin were not sensitive to heat, cold, pain Etck, Yuman Beans wld be much stoopider than they already are, and spend all their time cutting themselves, getting burnt Etck. All in all, we can pass a hearty vote of thanks for Skin, sez El Chubb. Thank you, Skin.

Normal Teenage Worrier's skin cont:

Flakey patch →   Red patch ↓   Cold sore ↓   GREASE ↓

(all on a fine layer of   PUSTULES)

SPORT

Yes! She's coming up on the inside! She's going faster and higher than any of the other competitors ... and ... here it comes! It MUST be the biggest! Let's just see whether the weighing and measuring team will confirm our assessment. They have! It's a Gold for the UK! Letty Chubb has won the First Olympic Nose-picking competition with the biggest, fattest bogey the werld has ever seen ...

I dread to think what the drugs rools wld be for this kind of competition. Can you put steroids into bogeys?

Many of you may have turned the page in disgust, but I draw attention to my only chance of winning an Olympic medal for the following reason: although many of our Sporty types often dream of Olympic wins, they have V. Little chance of achieving this aim in these islands, as Sports facilities in Brit skules are V. Poor and teachers are now so overworked by National Curriculum Etck, that they are unlikely to give up their Saturdays like they used to, to whip their lanky, knobbly, stubby, unwilling adolescents into vibrant teams of fresh-faced energy.

However, Sport is prob more popular now than it has ever been, prob because there is so much of it on TV. Yoof who can't find a job want something that gives them Respeck if they can't get Dosh so they Work Out Etck, and it seems like a quick way to

Stand up: the ratfink who invented the PE kit

get V. Famous if you practice enough to be V. Good at it. Gurlz are also getting into Sports that previously used only to be done by Boyz, including Football. El Chubb thinks that, though Sport can be V. Competitive and Aggressive, it brings Teenage Worriers together and allows you to meet and have fun with people you hardly know or might not otherwise meet. It is also V. Good for the skin, muscles, fitness Etck. It used to be popular with Grown Ups as something that wld stop Teenagers thinking about SEX, but I reckon with all those gleaming muscles, tight shorts, lurex jumpsuits Etck on Gladiators the opposite is usually true.

Anyway, Teenage Worriers Unite, campaign for better Sports in skule!

See also EXERCISE, FOOTBALL.

SPOT-SCRUTINIZING

Essential items for this LIFE activity are:

1) Spots
2) Mirror.

Many tragick hours can be whiled away on this LIFE-extinguishing activity. If I counted the hours I have spent bemoaning cratered mug and think how many novels, paintings Etck I might have created, or useful service to the community I might have

If your skin is this bad, you can always look on the bright side and play join the dots

performed . . . But such maundering only leads to more glume and more glume leads to more feverish Spot-Scrutinizing. This is what is meant, we think, by a Vicious Circle.

L. CHUBB'S SPOT TIPS:

1) Do not squeeze them. This advice is impossible to follow unless you wear

    a) A straitjacket

    b) Concrete mittens.

So, if you must, only squeeze the blackheads.

2) Wash face twice a day with antiseptic soap.

3) If they go on and on and on, see doc. Try Chinese herbs. Do not despair. 70% of Teenagers get Spots. They will go eventually.

4) Instead of scrutinizing yr own Spots, try scrutinizing other people's. Obviously do this in subtle, caring way, else they will be V. Hurt – eg: take sneaky look, pretending you are admiring shape of their mouth or hooter. NB Do not assume that if anyone is observing shape of *yr* mouth or hooter that they are neccessarily counting yr Spots.

5) Consider changing breed from 'Person' to 'Dalmatian'.

6) Wear balaclava.

292

SURGERY

Cosmetic surgery is now another Worry for Manhattan Babes with loadsadosh. Luckily it is not a Worry *moi* can afford to have and it's one American obsession I really hope stays the other side of Atlantic as far as Teenagers are concerned. We have enough on plate Etck. It's all done by stretching and cutting yr skin yeeeech or implanting collagen (cow fat). There is no long-term research on this and no long-term improvements, either (about 6 months before you need new collagen – arg). People think they can get rid of fat by eating loads and having liposuction. This hoovers your fat off (V. Painful, they say) but where does the fat go? It sneaks off to gather elsewhere like yr forehead or something. Silicone's for bazooms (you WANT a foreign body in you? Only if he's V. Handsome). And some surgeons are offering to make Asian people look European by offering double eyelids! Per-LEASE.

See APPEARANCES and IMAGE.

Plastic Surgeon

ROMAN NOSES a speciality

SUPERMODEL (daft new word for model)

Gurlz often want to be models. Clearly this is an unrealistic aim.

Why? 'Cos you have to be a beanpole. If you are short or plump or have anything normal about you at all (like normally squashy nose, normally crooked teeth, mouth, eyes, Etck) you have no chance. Only abnormal Gurlz are models. And they then have to work V. Hard to stay abnormal. 6 hours in the gym and dangerous starvation are part of this 'regime'.

Still, *Yoo-Hoo!*, *Weenybop*, *Smirk* Etck pander so this notion by running competitions for 'Hopefuls' who then starve themselves, iron their wigs, get plastic surgery Etck, in order to earn a fortune.

BE WARNED: if you think it would be fun being a clothes horse who's forced to do exactly what a horde of overpaid photographers and underpaid make-up Gurlz and overpaid fashion editors tell her, then fine. One of you may end up rich, if you are abnormal enough. Also bear in mind that if you *are* V. Byootiful, then you don't need to try to become a Supermodel just to get people to notice you Etck; they will do that anyway (snivel, jealous rage Etck). If you *want* to be a model more than anything else in the world, that's different.

BUT do avoid ads offering you portfolios of photos for a fee. These are either seedy, or a rip-off. Make sure you only go to V. V. Reputable agency.

SWEAT

Sweat is OK these days, even for Gurlz. It is, of course, V. Nachural function that stops yr Bod overheating like a car with no radiator, but it has usually been considered slightly Dodgy aspect of Yuman LIFE, which is why perlite people called it Perspiration instead, and a whole industry turned up to hide the smell, marks on clothes Etck, as if people didn't really sweat at all.

With the return of much interest in Body Culchur, werking out, muscle-building (for both Boyz and Gurlz) Etck, Sweat as rather attractive steamy sheen on polished Bods has become OK. It only smells if you don't wash it off every day, or don't wash it out of yr clothes. Teenage Worriers, who often think laundry is something Adored Parents or other slaves are there to do, sometimes ignore these things if Adored Parents, slaves Etck rebel or forget and don't do it. Then you begin to be aware of people moving away from you to other side of room Etck. This is not a good way to make new frendz, espesh of Opposite SEX (Boyz all together often don't seem to notice it, or maybe even enjoy it as macho ritual), so bear it in mind.

CHAPTER TWELVE
TTTTTTTTEEEEEEEze to
WWWWWWWz

First thing a.m. police say they have traced car to address in Suffolk and are calling round today.

Joy unconfined.

Race to meet Adam before skule.

He is not at skule gates, but wait patiently for an hour and less patiently for a further hour and V. Tragickly for a further hour. In pouring rain. Do not have heart to go to skule two hours late again. Must be some explanation. Must get home to see if any news of Only Mother, anyway.

Arrive home to find it surprisingly cheerful. Granny Chubb, kettle Etck singing merrily in grate, and a gleaming sheen of tidiness suffusing each surface with a well-scrubbed, welcoming glow. Had not realized true colour of kitchen floor till now. Not greyish-green after all, but rather pleasant honey tone.

Police arrived at Suffolk house to find woman answering description of Only Mother who shiftily refused to confirm same and said they couldn't come in without a warrant.

I can't believe it. We have found her (thanks to El Chubb, super-sleuth) and she doesn't want to be found! Not even a word of comfort for her Only Children!!

My despair is deepened by the following note which Granny Chubb had propped beside my pillow. It had arrived this morning just after I left.

Dear Scarlett,

I have heard of your affair with Daniel Hope, a person I profoundly despise. Clearly you feel differently and that is your choice. I have decided to take my chance in Los Angeles, where I have been invited to do a Summer Job in Mogul Mogul Junior the Third's studio. Obviously it was a job that held no interest for me while I thought you cared. But now that I know differently, I shall follow my worst instincts and hope to learn the tricks of the trade which I then may use in some way that will help purge the memory of this experience.

As you know, fame and wealth are not on my agenda. But film-making skills are — and I hope to learn them in this environment. I was disappointed to see the use to which you put your beautiful photographs — I had thought better of you.

But I wish you happiness.

By the time you get this, I will be on my way. It is not cowardice that makes me write rather than meet you, but realism.

I know when I'm losing.

Yours,

Adam.

My AFFAIR with Daniel?
Who told him I was even SEEING Daniel? It must

have been Aggy! She was the only person who knew! But why would she do such a thing? And what did he mean about my photographs? So many questions remain unanswered but all I know are three Terrible Truths:

1) I have lost Adam because of my stupid faith in Daniel, who has now proved himself beyond the pale for ever.

2) I have been betrayed again by Aggy, whom I really trusted.

3) Last and Worst: my parents are splitting up.

This LIFE has become a Vale of Tears, Slough of Despond, Pain Without End Etck. Have written to Mother Theresa asking if I can help out in Calcutta, or possibly join Starving Poor as hostage to take my mind off myself.

Tanning

Tanning is becoming unKool owing to skin cancer from sun's rayz. Advice: Wear a Big Hat. Wear good sunglasses so as not to fry your eyes. Wear factor 22. Put it on every two hours or so. But you can take it too far: Ashley went to interview someone of 70 for his skule magazine once. She had stayed indoors for most of her LIFE to avoid sun-ageing. He said she didn't look a day over 69. Sad.

TEENAGE THINK TANK

ABOVE: Just a few examples of the SCORN poured
on the inventions of Teenage Worriers

CAMPAIGN! For a TEENAGE THINK TANK
to transform LIFE as we know it...

TEETH

All over World, Teenage Worriers are gnashing
what remains of their Toothy-pegs and
remembering tragickly their early visits to dentist,
who used to give them balloons and badges for 'star
teeth' Etck and who told them to brush twice a day.
But did they follow dentist's advice? Did they get
that brush up into the corners? Did they use the
right brush??? And why – despite endless warblings
of 'All I want for Christmas is my two front teeth' –
were they rewarded with the crumbly yellow fangs
they are currently lumbered with?

Fact is, if you don't look after your Teeth, they
will not look after you. But a lot of Tooth Stuff (like
so much else in LIFE, sigh) is hereditary and it's sad
but true that some thrice daily brushers are left with
krap snappers and vicey versy.

Also, Tooth shape is hardly your fault (though
dummies do less harm than thumb-sucking
apparently . . . but it's too late for you to think of
that now, except for your own offspring). If you need
braces, why not colour co-ordinate them with yr
socks? All sorts of colours available nowadays. Don't
get *too* hung up on Teeth. Strong and healthy is
better than straight and white and lots of the best
faces have quirky fangs. The Americans spend
fortunes on their mouths, and so will you if you
leave it too late as NHS dentists are fast
disappearing. Get stuff fixed early while you're

entitled to Free dentistry. After than, grin and bear
it (or perhaps that shld be smirk and don't bare
them?).

TRAINERS

Museums of the future will be V. Interesting places
for footwear. Future fok will ask: Did twentieth-
century BritKids actually wear that stuff? But while
Trainers are obv V. Much more sensible Etck than
Stilettos, their prices are certainly not. Wot, I ask
you, are we paying £90 for? A label? An 'air
bubble'? Silver laces? LIGHTS? Per-LEASE. I have,
like all Teenage Worriers, done my share of
yearning for *Tike Vampires*, complete with
retractable roller-blade, CD player, automatic kick-
yer-enemy-into-next-year function Etck Etck. But I
ponder ye economics and I have regrettably to say
there are better things (fudge, G. Chubb's glasses)
on which to spend the dosh. 'Course, if they invent a
pair with WINGS, then I'll be singing a different
toon. So far, they have only put wings on sanitary
towels and these, as far as I can see, do not need to
fly.

Then there's the added Fashion-Worry of LACES.
Yurg. It's bad enuf when you are 7 and have to
change for PE and you are the only child in class
who can't do its laces up and your horrible parent
has forgotten that you begged to wear velcro shoes.

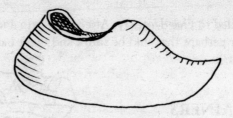

If beset by Trainer-Worry,
why not consider the humble clog?

Or El Chubb's Jester-Boot (patent pending)

When you are a Teenage Worrier it gets a whole lot
worse, as you have to lace 'em horizontally, only
using one half of the laces, or lace them top-to-
bottom missing out centre holes, or wear the laces
just round your ankles. See how fickle changing
fashion is? Buy cheapo slip-on plimsolls and avoid
this fashion Worry. El Chubb predicts you will start
a new Superkool wave.

See FASHION.

TRANSPORT

Getting Around is a Big Prob for Teenage Worriers, due to lack of dosh, inability to drive Etck. It is usually necessary to call up Adored Parents minicab service, which they particularly dislike when summoned 30 miles to some scuzzy klub in the middle of the night.

If you live in London, tubes are OK and not *too* expensive as long as you get right Travelcards Etck and have big advantage for Geographical Dyslexics like *moi*, in that they TELL YOU WHERE YOU ARE. Why don't bus stops have names on like tube stations? It wld be so much easier. (Thinks: Cld create a bus map like the tube map and make fortune.)

An e.g. of my sympathetic folks?

In fact, most Teenage Worriers out late generally prefer the buses, which can be qu. nice sociable places to travel around: there's something to look at if you end up having seething silent row with Person you're travelling with; they run later at night; and they have V. Big advantage of not being full of looooong echoing corridors empty except for lurking muggers Etck.

Late travel on public transport, however, is an opportunity to see the Adult Werld at its worst, and it is V. Diff to see how the Older Generation can be qu. so fussy about Terrible Teenage Habitz when you realize how many of them are staggering around the city barely able to stand.

Avoid traffic chaos –
learn to ride a unicycle

If you live in a country district, travel and transport is a V. Big Prob indeed, and you are usually forced to rely on Adored Parents and Parents' frendz with cars, which can restrict yr freedom and sense you are growing up into a proper autonomous Person. But much better to put up with that than walk alone in deserted districts at night, or try to hitch lifts. These can turn out in some cases to be frightening or even dangerous activities, and are Not Recommended by El Urban-Groover Chubb, even though she thinks a stile is deciding to wear a bin-liner with a plastic tiara Etck.

Obviously ye trusty bicycle is V. Imp for most of us, but El Chubb stresses importance of right safety gear, fluorescent belts, cycling hats Etck — better to look nerdish than . . . er, meet the Grim Reaper. Also, it just isn't safe to cycle in busy cities unless there's a proper track. Campaign for cyclists' pavements that are as safe as pedestrians' pavements!

TRAVELLERS

Folk-lore will describe the Gypsy thus: Dastardly, beggarly n'er-do-wells who steal innocent children. Also, V. Romantick curly-haired ear-ringed Lurvers who whisk you away to rural idyll. As usual, Opinion-formers take one view, and Teenage Worriers take the other. Truth, inevitably, lies in between. So if yr Gypsy Lurver brings out the Gypsy in yr Soul but the fascist in yr father, take heed. Age and wisdom do count for *something* and it may be that your aged parent discerns a less than worthy soul beneath the glittering surface. (Goodness, is this *moi* speaking? Why am I giving such measured

Could this be the gypsy in my soul? Swooon...

Advice? – Because, dear Reader, I have been Betrayed. And I have seen my Mother Betrayed. And I have seen my Father Betrayed – his Gypsy was Spangly Angy, who ditched him for the snake charmer.)

Real-LIFE Gypsies, of course, are Romany Travellers, who are sadly being routed from our countryside by an Uncaring Govt. These are distinct from New Age Travellers, who are just like you and me but prefer a LIFE on the open road. This seems like a V. Good option in today's uncaring werld of shrinking council housing, huge mortgages and huger rents. And, given latest statistics of homeless young people, it seems like that's what most of us

308

are being forced into anyway. I wld rather try to get hold of a small horse and cart and a tent than live on the Strand in a cardboard box . . .

SUPPORT GYPSIES! FREE CAMPING FOR ALL! (this handy two-in-one slogan also to apply to Gay Campaigns).

VEGETARIANISM

Large numbers of V. sensible Caring Teenage Worriers have become Vegetarians of late. Their numbers were doubled by the BSE scare and quadrupled by *Babe*, the V. cute film about a talking piggy which put Benjy off sausages for a whole day. There are some good arguments for and against this: If we didn't raise any sheep or cattle we wouldn't have much grass; it would all be given over to other crops and the countryside wld look V. Different. On

the other hand, it is V. Uneconomic for the world to get so much of its protein from meat (soya wld produce more protein more cheaply) and modern methods of factory farming are extremely cruel and, it now seems, possibly very harmful to ye food chain.

Also if you are still growing, it is V.V.V. Imp to get enough protein, which requires a bit of thought if you are a Vegetarian. Most veggies eat some animal products which do not involve killing animals – ie: eggs, butter, milk, cheese: all V. Good for protein, as are nuts and soya beans. I feel I shld be a Vegetarian, but instead have been perswading Only Mother to buy organic meat and free range chickens. More expensive but at least you know they've had a happy LIFE.

See DIET.

VIDEOS

Last month we became last family in Little Britain to rent a Video Recorder. So now, if Adored Mother and Father get back together again and have A Celebration Treat (which they do only normally once about every 50 million years) they'll be like everyone else: they'll rent a Video and get an Indian takeaway. If this is an example to Us Yoof about how to live LIFE to the full, drink deep of the cup of Yuman Experience, climb every mountain, dare to

LIVE and dare to cry Etck, then the sooner those people who keep saying the World's going to end on Tuesday week get their way the better.

I'd always rather see the films that I really like in the cinema, because once you've seen them there watching them at home is like listening to Rachmaninov's Third Piano Concerto played on a xylophone. Videos can, of course, be useful for watching stuff you're not supposed to. I went round to Hazel's house one night when her parents were out and she had a Video called *Wild Awakening*, which was about a Boy and Gurl sounding as if they're having asthma attacks most of the time, and tearing at each other's zips, buttons Etck on buses, in public loos, behind bushes, in cars Etck Etck. I was V. Excited by all this for a bit, but after a while we switched it off and played Scrabble instead.

I do find Videos are one area of Home LIFE where us Teenage Worriers can get a bit of control of the situation. This is because many Adored Parents can't understand new electronic Video Machines and tellys and tear up the instructions in Video Rage Etck, so it's often us who are the only ones who know how to work it all. Akshully, having been V. Keen to join herd and get one of these, I have trouble with it *moi*self, but I leave it to Benjy who understands it by instinct, and then pretend it was me.

VIRTUAL REALITY

In case you hadn't noticed, komputer graphics are getting so good these days they almost look like film, and imitation of Reality has become V. Amazing, making screen games Etck much more exciting than they used to be. This has led to the opening of huge Virtual Reality centres and theme parks, where Teenage Worriers are to be found spending a lot of time and dosh careering around Virtual racetracks, down Virtual ski-slopes, through Virtual battlefields Etck.

Development of this technology now goes on so fast that what is Mind-boggling one year is Dead As Dodo the next, and it must be like Christmas every day for the makers of this Stuff, because the Effex are constantly changed and people don't get bored. People grow out of it instead, though in the case of my Adored Father this is not true, and when we all went to Hyperwerld once, he was the one who wouldn't leave.

But El Chubb has to confess to being bored by a lot of this Stuff and when she tried the Virtual ski-slope she had to be led away with panic attacks. Benjy, however, despite the fact the floor was constantly disappearing from under him, loved every minute of it and it might turn out to be V. Good aversion therapy for his phobia, although almost as expensive as hiring a private head-doctor. For *moi*self, I would like to see a Virtual Romance game, where you could give the machine a pic of Yr Elusive BeLurved, and it immediately creates a steamy satin-sheets scenario with the Person of Yr Dreamz and you together in it, doing Whatever You Want (pant, sigh, heave Etck). I fear, however, that if this came to pass, you might end up feeling a bit Seedy that the Person wasn't really there to go and have a Strawberry Milkshake with afterwards. But then maybe if Virtual Reality got that good, they *would* be.

Teenage Worry factor No. 543: How would we then know who was the Real Person and who

wasn't? Would it matter? Would the Real People just stay at home in a kind of fridge, while Virtual Clones of them went out and Did Thingz? Will this be clutched on to by Werld Govts as way of solving food shortage, crime wave Etck? Answers to Teenage Think Tank please . . .

Tidy up a boy scout TODAY!

VOLUNTEERING

V. Good to do werk for nothing for people who have even less than Teenage Worriers. Our local charity shop was closed for two days before Christmas this year (just when they could be doing really well) because of lack of Volunteers. Yeeeeech, guilt. Two hours a week doing something V. Caring is Good for Soul, sez *moi*. Must make it New Year's Resolution for year 20000.

Walking

What? El Chubb donning boots made out of bits of Stonehenge and toting horrible rucksack through mud and brambles in hearty manner? No fear. I prefer a short walk to the chip shop, but we're all different and I do have a sneaky admiration for those V. Energetic healthy types who storm off over hill and dale whistling a happy tune. In Olden Times like the 1950s, it seems people used to think this sort of thing was V. Good for combating the onset of Sekshul Urrrrges in Teenage Worriers, or even for stopping them becoming Worriers at all, because they wld be bursting with Godz Fresh Air, brains pulsating with oxygen, capable of no more at night than falling into a dreamless, fantasyless sleep as soon as they hit the pillow. Reluctantly, I am forced to admit that exercise is prob. V. Good for mental energy, optimism Etck, but personally I wld rather dance, train to become Gladiator, take up karate Etck than clump around the countryside in jumper made from about 50 sheep, with half the contents of my room on my back.

On *le autre main*, walking V. Good for body, soul, environment Etck (guilt, lash).

FINAL CHAPTER
XXXXXXes to ZZZZZZze

Look, I'm glad to say a lot's unravelled since my last chapter — most of it is pretty good and some of it is terrible. The terrible thing was that Sleeve SOLD my photos to the horrible tabloid newspaper the Slob *so that Aggy was plastered all over the centre spread as an image of a typical poor, black Londoner. What was worse, they retouched the pics to make it look as if she was surrounded by about a hundred babies, plus nicked tellys, mobile phones Etck and showing her knickers as well.*

The paper banged on about how there were too many people like Aggy and they were SPONGING OFF THE WELFARE STATE, causing Tidal Wave of Crime Etck. I couldn't believe it.

Not surprisingly, Aggy had thought it was ME who sold the pictures and had immediately told Adam I was seeing Daniel. I don't blame her, not one bit. I can't even get Sleeve, because he had bought the pictures off me with an 'Option' (which I didn't understand, of course, but now realize means Option to Stitch Up Dumb Artist Etck). But his name will be MUD for ever, or Merde, as the Euros say.

I have written to Adam explaining everything, but I didn't lie about Daniel, and he hasn't written back. He probably has discovered by now that Candice Cleavage (I

mean Carthage) is a Better Person than her father
(apparently her first film was amazingly good and all
about the Urban Poor . . .) and definitely a Better Person
than moi.

The really GOOD news, though, is that my Mother
was not seeing the ex-student-turned-komputer-wizard
after all! 'Neville' was a happily married tutor on the
komputer graphics course whose WIFE had invited my
Mother over for a few days to discuss starting up a small
business! Mother had left a message on the ansaphone
about it and had also written Dad a note, viz:

Sweetheart,
    Buzzing off for a couple of days to make loads of dosh
(I hope) so we can all be comfy again. I'll be staying with
Vera Snythe and her husband Neville at {then she gives
the Suffolk address}. Have left half a sausage roll in
fridge. Will ring tonite.
    All love.

Unfortunately, my Mother, being in a bit of a tizz,
had left Neville's note to her on the table and put her note
to Dad in her handbag. Arg.

My Father, having the gadget wizardry of a
technically challenged amoeba (as proved by his only ever
getting to level 2 of the kiddies' game CITYSCAPE,
despite pretending otherwise) had managed to disconnect
ansaphone and – after tearful call to Samaritans – had
not put our phone back on hook properly. Meanwhile police
had called on furious Mrs Snythe (who looks a bit like

Mother), who had no idea what they were talking about. She only pieced it together when she told Neville and my Mother about the police coming. My Mother had enrolled on the course as Ms Gosling and neglected to mention her relationship with my Adored Father. This had been my Only Mother's touching attempt to seem Young(ish) and Free of Responsibilities and therefore a dashing business partner for Mrs Snythe. Therefore police at door going on about missing wife of Leonard Chubb (which is how my demented Father referred to her) had naturally meant nothing to poor Mrs Snythe. When Mother heard about the police she put two and two together and surged home to find us all in mourning . . .

Well, not quite. We had by then discovered the joy of having Granny Chubb making boiled eggs and soldiers for us all and generally cosseting us more than we were accustomed to. After an initial moment of feeling hurt, my Only Mother made a tentative suggestion. Why didn't Granny Chubb move in? We could halve all our living expenses and have boiled eggs, cauliflower cheese and apple pie every day!

Rover, Benjy, Father and me Over Moon at this suggestion. And so, dear Readers, I am feeling V.V.V. Much better. I have explained ALL to Aggy (who believes me), and have enrolled in another film course as I am going to take my career prospects seriously now. We have divided the front room so Granny Chubb has her own space — shared for much of the time with Darling Father, for whom she is knitting a pair of bedsocks. Sharing space has proved economical and (blush), with a little help from guilt-stricken Only Father, I have finally saved enough in my GCSE fund to buy Granny Chubb a decent pair of specs. It's nice to have one *thing to be proud of. Also, does Coming of the Bedsock mean I will be saved from the Invasion of the Boleros? Anyway, it is touching to see how V.V. Happy she is.*

My Mother is now let off the domestick hook as G. Chubb does all the catering – and she is making headway with her business! And Dad got a nice review of his buke *in the poshest Sunday paper. Which means, according to his publisher, that the others will start, too.*

Benjy's floor phobia is in recession (either due to the stunning new cleanliness of said floors or possibly the comforting presence of G. Chubb). Maybe a rosy future beckons after all.

But one thing I have learnt, both from my use of Hazel's video and the SLOB's use of my photographs: sometimes, the camera CAN lie.

Xanadu

Where Kubla Khan decreed an ancient Pleasure Dome, according to ye poet Coleridge. V. Nice, if only he would decree a Pleasure Dome on each mean street inhabited by Teenage Worriers.

Year

YES

Ending on Happy Note dept.

Just say 'Yes' to LIFE, suggests L. Chubb. Explore all possibilities and do not be cowed by glumey cows like *moi* who preach dume. Make a list of all yr major Worries (er, keep a copy . . .). Then screw up list, tear into a thousand tiny pieces and scatter to the wind (I mean, put neatly in dustbin liner, to avoid litter-guilt). Your Worries have now disappeared. You can check the copy you kept two or three times a day to make sure you are not Worrying . . .

And after you've done all that, you can forget about ZODIACS, ZEBRAS, ZEUS, ZONES and just snoozzzzzzzzzze. . . .

One of LIFE'S burning questions: "Do fleas sleep?"

FILL IN NOW

If you want to...

Date:

Biggest **WORRIES**:

Biggest **HOPES**:

Best **PEOPLE**:

Best **THINGS**:

OTHER (worries, fears, hopes, dreams, loves, hates....)

PTO →

ONE YEAR LATER

Wait a year (YES! go on!) and then
fill this in (WITHOUT sneaking a look
at the page Before)

Date:

Biggest **WORRIES**:

Biggest **HOPES**:

Best **PEOPLE**:

Best **THINGS**:

OTHER (worries, fears, hopes, dreams,
loves, hates...)

V. Interesting to see if stuff is better,
worse or same. Gives, um, PERSPECTIVE
Etck. (IF WORSE, bound to get better,
cos that's **LIFE**).

Send this to me anytime you want – no
need to wait.

Dear Letty,
        I am   yrs old. Here are
some of the things I think the
TEENAGE THINK TANK
should consider:

Here are the things that I WORRY
about most in my own **LIFE**.

This is what would make me **HAPPY**.

        from:

Send to: Letty Chubb, TRANGWORLD,
        61-63 UXBRIDGE RD, LONDON
        W5 5SA.
(add more paper if you want).

THE TEENAGE 'WORRIER'S Guide to LURVE

by Ros Asquith

The Long-Awaited sequel to the best-selling
I WAS A TEENAGE WORRIER

Yes! Here it is! From moi, Letty Chubb, aged 15.
A thrusting, PASSIONATE, JUICY, (phew, must hurl
self into cold shower) Look at EVERY aspect
of LURVE.

'Hilarious... will help with any questions to do with
the L-word' *TV Hits*

'Good for a laugh and great advice' *The Times*

Only £4.99!!

0 552 14339 1

HELP!

Useful telephone numbers for serious LIFE worries...

CHILDLINE
Freephone 0800 1111
If you or a friend have been abused, these people will be very helpful and sympathetic.

THE SAMARITANS
National Linkline
0345 909090 (calls charged at local rate from wherever you call)
24-hour emergency service for the suicidal or despairing. A local number will also be in your telephone book or can be obtained by calling the operator. If in serious trouble, DO CALL.

ALATEEN (part of Al-Anon)
0171 403 0888
24-hour confidential helpline, specifically for teenagers affected by the drinking problem of a family member or friend.

DRINKLINE
Helpline: 0345 320202
Freephone 0500 801802
Confidential, national alcohol helpline. Very helpful with advice on drinking levels Etck. Free information packs.

DEPARTMENT OF HEALTH NATIONAL DRUGS HELPLINE
Freephone 0800 776600
A free and confidential service open 24 hours a day, 365 days a year. Also available in a range of languages other than English. Free leaflets and literature.

BROOK ADVISORY CENTRES
0171 713 9000 (helpline, office hours)
0171 617 8000 (recorded information helpline)
Contraceptive and counselling service for the under 25s. Local clinics throughout the UK. Under 16s can obtain confidential help.

The information above was correct at the time of going to press. If any errors occur, Transworld Publishers Ltd will be pleased to rectify at the earliest opportunity.

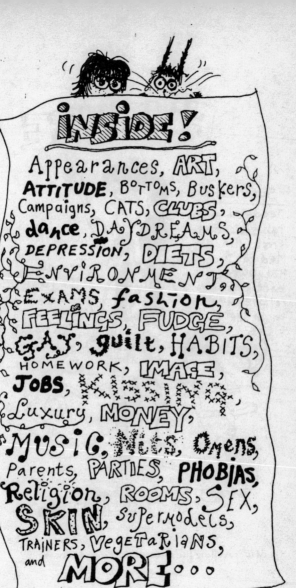

Moi: travelling lite towards the Great Unknown...